D0828735

OTHER BOOKS BY CHRISTINA A. BURKE

Queenie Baby:

Queenie Baby: On Assignment

Queenie Baby: Out of Office

Queenie Baby: Pass the Eggnog
(holiday novella)

QUEENIE BABY: ON ASSIGNMENT

a Queenie Baby novel

CHRISTINA A. BURKE

To my husband Jim, our children, and our family and friends.

And to all the other wacky characters I've met along the zigzag path of life.

CHAPTER ONE

——————

So I'm not technically a rock star—yet. In fact, "rock star" might even be too strong a term for my musical ambitions. My name is Diana Hudson, and I like to think of myself as a working musician. Only the reality is that sometimes I'm working as a musician, and sometimes I'm broke and working as a temp. Not exactly the most glamorous job, but it pays the bills between gigs.

My most recent assignment was as a personal assistant to a vampire. Okay, not a *real* vampire, but as close as this almost-rock star has ever seen. Of course, Carol didn't tell me I was being assigned to a vampire when she offered me the three-week position.

"He's a visiting professor from Yugoslavia," she explained. "You'll be working out of his hotel. A nice one. He's a little eccentric, but we've worked with him before. And he pays well."

She had me at "pays well." Besides, it sounded easy enough. Show up at 10:00 a.m., work until 4:00p.m. typing a manuscript—piece of cake, right?

A little bit about me. I live in Annapolis, Maryland, but I'm originally from a little town in southern Delaware. I had just turned thirty, no man in the picture unless you count my dog, Max, and, according to most of my family, no actual career. I'm freakishly tall, with long straight blond hair and blue eyes. I might be described as having a willowy kind of elegance if I weren't so clumsy. Think one part Grace Kelly and two parts Lucille Ball.

Anyway, back to the vampire. So I showed up at the hotel fifteen minutes ahead of time, dressed in a professional Banana Republic pantsuit. He answered the door wearing—no lie—a black cape. His hair was flowing salt and pepper with a high widow's peak. His skin was a chalky white.

"You must be Miss Hudson," he drawled. "Please come in."

Actually, he wasn't as creepy as you might think. He was handsome in an old guy way. Distinguished and gentlemanly. I took a quick look around his suite. The hotel was a small, upscale boutique-style building in the historic district. The kind of place that attracted people with yachts. Posh furnishings, although a little stuffy for my tastes. And thankfully, no sign of a coffin.

I'd been temping for five years. The last three I'd spent working almost exclusively for Carol Smith at Greene's Staffing Services. Carol took great care of me. I rarely went a week without work. I made sure to be on time, dress professionally, and not act crazy in front of the clients. Job requirements that seemed to stump many temporaries, according to Carol. And since I live two blocks from the office, most mornings I'd drop by with coffee and Carol's favorite pastry, monkey bread from Shack's Bakery. A little bribery never hurt when looking for the prime jobs.

As a seasoned temp, not much surprised me anymore.

Not the weird jobs—I once delivered mail to Baltimore prisons. Yep, Baltimore.

Or the eccentric employers—I once worked for a CEO at a manufacturing company who designated his office as the official break room, so he could smoke at his desk all day.

Not even the curiosities of my many short-term co-workers—like being excluded from partaking in office birthday cake because of my temporary status. Yes, seriously.

But a guy in a cape was new.

"Hello, Mr. Pyres," I began. "Carol said you need help with a manuscript while you're in town."

He turned with a flourish. The cape billowed out around him. He floated over to a desk piled high with books and papers. I tried really hard to remain professional and not burst into a round of pre-pubescent giggles.

"Make yourself comfortable," he said, indicating the high back upholstered chair in front of the desk. "And please, call me Vann."

I raised an eyebrow but said nothing. Really? Vann Pyres? I settled myself into the chair and crossed my legs.

"Did Miss Smith mention that my writing process is rather different?" he asked with a quirky nod of encouragement.

I shook my head "no."

"Well, you see, I study medieval literature, and I like to keep with the old ways so to speak."

Like a chisel and stone tablet? I bit back. No, just nod in agreement.

He reached across the desk and pulled out a quill pen from an antique ink well. He waved the pen around like he was conducting an orchestra.

"Miss Hudson, I tell you, this is the only way to write!" Spit flew from his lips.

He gathered himself and said with a sigh, "Alas, my publisher refuses to accept anything unless it has been fed into that executioner of human dignity—the computer!"

I swear I think I heard Dark Shadow's organ music as he finished.

"This is where your services come in," he said with a slight smile. "I need you to type up my manuscript on a *computer*." He could barely choke out the word. "I can't abide those things in my presence, so you will have to work in the executive office space provided by the hotel."

With what should have won me a place in the Temp Hall of Fame, I smiled brightly and said, "Sounds like an interesting project! I can't wait to get started."

* * *

Six hours and a dozen spindly handwritten pages later, I was headed back to my car, a well-preserved Honda Civic. It was warm for early April, so I drove the short distance with the windows down and my iPod tuned to Jack Johnson. God, what I wouldn't give for some banana pancakes right now. But I had business to attend to. First stop was Carol. She had some explaining to do. "The Count," as I'd taken to calling Mr. Pyres, was fairly easy to work with. That didn't, however, change the fact that Carol had sent me in blind on this assignment. Second stop, the bar down the street from my condo. Pancakes could wait. There was a martini calling my name.

I found a parking space strategically located between the agency and my condo. It was a good space. No way would this have happened in the summer. My condo had zero parking, especially during the day, or anytime at the height of the tourist season. Most evenings I was able to find a space close by. In the summer I rented a space in a lot three blocks away.

Greene's Staffing Service was located in a storefront in the business district. It was sandwiched between Nails 2Go and Spellbound, a Wiccan specialty store that seemed to sell more pot paraphernalia than pentacles. The sidewalk in front of Greene's was tidy with an old-fashioned green awning over the doorway. Through the big glass windows I could see Carol in a heated discussion with another temp. I pulled the old wood and glass door open and stepped inside.

"There isn't anything to discuss, Angela," said Carol patiently. "You were three hours late for your first day at Dr. Mason's office. And when you finally got there you wanted to know when lunch was. He doesn't want you back."

"Well, it was lunch time, wasn't it?" replied Angela with a roll of her eyes. "So what—I'm not supposed to eat?"

Looked to me like Angela had been eating just fine, but I kept my mouth shut. Carol was a master at these situations.

"Angela, you went to school to be a medical office assistant. You know you have to show up on time. The patients are depending on you."

"All I know, Miss Carol, is that this is your fault!" Angela exclaimed and shook a long red acrylic nail emblazoned with the Red Cross symbol at Carol.

Carol stared at her blankly for a second. Her eyes were magnified through her thick glasses. With bobbed brown hair and almost no makeup Carol looked middle-aged, but I couldn't even begin to guess how old she really was. The glasses made her look a bit like a wise old owl.

I couldn't wait to watch her deal with this one.

Cool as can be, Carol asked, "And how's that?"

"Well, you told me to look nice and professional."

"Yes, I did," Carol agreed.

Now whether or not Angela looked nice and professional was up for debate.

"Look at my nails." Angela flashed them around Carol's face. "And look at my hair. Do you know how long it takes to get hair like this?" Angela patted her pink braided weave that rose six inches off her head and cascaded in braids down her back. Tiny lime-green beads on the ends clacked with every shake of her head.

Carol remained silent.

Angela rolled on. "I've been up since five this mornin'. My hairdresser got me in special just for this new job. An' you tellin' me that bougie doctor don't want me back?"

"That's correct," replied Carol.

Now at this point things could go either way. Carol was either going to get told to fuck off, or Angela was going to cry and ask for a second chance. My bet was Angela was going for a second chance. After all, she'd just gotten her hair done, right?

"Oh, please give me a second chance, Miss Carol," Angela wailed. "I want to be a medical office assistant. You know I got good grades in all my classes. Can't you call the doctor back?" Angela's braids clanged noisily as she sobbed.

Carol handed her a tissue from the strategically placed box. "No," she said, "I'm not calling Dr. Mason back, and this *was* your second chance. Remember what happened at the clinic last month?"

Angela blew her nose. "That bitch had it comin'. She been messin' with my baby daddy and comes into the clinic where I'm workin' to get a pregnancy test? Oh, hell no!"

"You threw urine at her," Carol reminded her.

"Yeah, but it was hers. It's not like I threw some stranger's urine at her."

Oops—Angela just blew it with Carol. 'Fess up and apologize, and Carol would work with you. Defend throwing urine on your baby daddy's ho at the free clinic, and you were terminated.

"I'm sorry, Angela, but we will no longer be able to place you." Carol extended her hand in a smooth move I'd seen her use with a dozen others. Keep one hand busy in case they tried to swing at you. "I wish you the best in your career," she said with a sympathetic smile.

Angela shook her hand. I had never seen anyone refuse Carol. It was almost compulsive to shake someone's hand, and Carol knew it. It also made people less likely to punch you in the face afterwards.

Angela tossed her head and spun around towards the door. In a clattering of braids and beads she was gone.

"Another satisfied customer," I said.

"Yeah, it's been one of those days. Two no call-no shows and Angela." She shook her head.

"Oh, you haven't heard about my day yet."

Carol eyed me warily and held up her hand. "I know, I know. He handwrites everything. No fun, but he pays well. It's a good job."

"He's a vampire, Carol," I said. "You sent me to work for a vampire."

"Don't be ridiculous," she said waving her hand dismissively.

"The man was wearing a cape," I said.

Carol looked a little uncomfortable. "He's still got the cape, huh?"

"*Still* got the cape! Really? A little warning would have been appreciated," I sputtered. Okay, I don't mind crappy or crazy assignments if they pay well, but Carol usually gave me plenty of warning. "So what's the deal? The guy's name is Vann Pyres, and he wears a black cape, and you don't think to mention it?" I said.

"I thought he was done with the cape. And besides, you've been on so many challenging assignments that I thought you could handle him," Carol said.

"It doesn't bother you in the least that this guy is crazy?" I asked. "Who did you send him last time?" I was getting suspicious.

Carol stalled by grabbing the ringing phone and giving me the one-sec finger. "Sure, Mr. Greene. Yes, that would be fine. Tomorrow? You'll be here? In the office?" For a split second Carol's impenetrable professional mask dropped, and I saw panic. "Yes, I'm looking forward to finally meeting you. Wonderful. You too, bye." Carol hung up the phone and stared at it for a few seconds.

"Why the stricken look? So your boss is coming into the office tomorrow," I said with a shrug. "It's not like he's a vampire or anything."

She didn't even crack a smile at my timely joke.

"I've never met him before," she said.

"Didn't he hire you for this job?" I asked.

"*Old* Mr. Greene hired me. I had quarterly conference calls with old Mr. Greene and monthly calls with his accountant; I haven't seen old Mr. Greene since the 2010 Boat Show. He lives somewhere in Virginia. *Young* Mr. Greene, his nephew, is coming tomorrow." She frowned, chewing her lip with a nervous nibble.

"How bad can he be?" I asked.

"He said old Mr. Greene is semi-retiring and has asked him to do an appraisal of the business and the property. To me, that sounds like either I have a new boss, or they're thinking of selling the place. "

"So no big deal," I tried to assure her. "You'll just have calls with young Mr. Greene now."

"What if he decides to sell the business?" she said.

"Well, that's thinking on the bright side," I replied. "Hey, come with me to McGlynn's for happy hour. Have a drink. Get relaxed."

"Are you kidding? I've got work to do!" Carol said. "This place is a wreck, and I have to compile the first quarter reports. Oh God, I hope the numbers are good." She sounded slightly manic.

I left Carol worrying over her numbers after extracting a promise from her that if the numbers looked good she would be over. I wasn't holding my breath. Might as well go home and change.

I walked to my renovated condo/apartment on Calvert Street. It was located in an older section of West Annapolis. The house was a hundred years old. Large and boxy, with no old-fashioned charm at all. It was a casualty of the real estate boom. With high hopes, a wannabe flipper had purchased the vacant property in 2007. He had attempted to convert the 4,000-square-foot space into three luxury condos. He successfully completed the bottom two before ending up in foreclosure. Another flipper came behind him and picked the property up for fifty cents on the dollar. This flipper decided to turn the unfinished three-bedroom luxury penthouse into two utilitarian condos. I bought the one-bedroom for a reasonable price. I didn't miss the high end fixtures that my downstairs neighbors enjoyed. Knowing my mortgage was a fraction of theirs was enjoyment enough.

How does a musician/temp afford to buy anything? No, I didn't have a hit song or land a year-long assignment running a hedge fund. My sister and I inherited half of our Great Aunt Sarah's estate a couple of years ago. I only met my great aunt a few times, but she never had children or cats, so I guess we were it. I used the money to put enough down on my condo, so that my mortgage would always be affordable. My sister inherited the other half and promptly bought the most ostentatious double-wide she could find and plopped it on a two-acre lot a mile from our old neighborhood. If you could call a line of boxes on a road between two dusty fields a neighborhood, that is.

As I approached my building, I saw my downstairs neighbor, Mrs. Kester, outside and obviously waiting for me. Her arms were crossed in front her, her sun-shriveled face pursed in a frown. The other unit on the first floor had been for sale for almost six months. The previous tenant had been a sweet, little old lady whose family had placed her in a nursing home. She had passed away a few months later. The real estate agent alluded to a family squabble over the estate as being responsible for the unit still being on the market. I had another theory. Mrs. Kester was old, but she definitely wasn't sweet, and she despised her neighbors. If she had her way, the whole building would be vacant. I think she had squashed more than one sale with her tales of out of control mold and corroded plumbing. The two-bedroom unit across from me was rented out during the tourist season. The steady flow of new tenants kept things interesting in the building during the summer and had Mrs. Kester foaming at the mouth from Memorial Day to Labor Day.

"Miss Hudson," she began, "I understand that you are used to living like a punk rock star."

I glanced down at my suit. So this is what punk rock looked like a hundred years ago.

"But I would appreciate it if you told your gentlemen callers to wait until they are in your apartment before removing their trousers," she continued.

Now, if Mrs. Kester had jumped on a broom and flown around the block, I wouldn't have been more surprised.

"There's a man with no pants outside my condo?" I asked incredulously. "Maybe you should have called the police!"

"Well, when I hollered at him, he said he knew you. And he called you by a rather familiar name," she said with a snooty sniff. "He's quite rude and much too old for you, but obviously that's none of my concern."

I walked through the front door warily, a horrifying thought crossing mind. I heard him before I saw him.

"Well, there's my Queenie Baby!" he exclaimed throwing open his arms and waving what looked like a wet pair of pants at me. "Come give me some sugar!"

Mrs. Kester was right on my heels. "Obviously someone you know."

"Yes," I ground out.

At the top of the stairs, stood a gray-haired, stooped man of eighty-two wearing no pants. Luckily he had on a red flannel shirt that hung down far enough to cover his parts. Strike that—most of his parts. He had a long white beard and looked for all the world like the crazy old coot he was. Granddaddy Hacker was on my doorstep.

I was going to kill my sister!

CHAPTER TWO

I opened the door to my condo and ushered Granddaddy Hacker inside, away from Mrs. Kester's disapproving looks. Although it looked like she might have been trying to check out Granddaddy's package—ewwh!

"What's wrong with your pants?" I asked.

"Had a little accident when I was waterin' your flowers out back," he cackled.

I gave him an evil look. "Watering?"

"I had to go, and that old bitty downstairs wasn't gonna let me in to use her facilities."

I took a deep, cleansing breath. Which unfortunately didn't do much to get rid of the old, naked guy. If I didn't get that drink soon, I wasn't sure I could be responsible for my actions.

After I insisted Granddaddy borrow a pair of my sweat pants, I settled him on the couch with a remote control in one hand and a piece of beef jerky in the other. Then I started the washer and added extra detergent.

"Got anymore jerky?" Granddaddy asked, never taking his eyes off the TV.

I put my hands on my hips. "No more jerky until you answer some questions!"

He ignored my request. "My dear Jenny always kept the shelves stocked. Couldn't cook worth a damn, but she made sure I had my jerky. Got it at a bargain too," he added wistfully.

Now I don't normally keep beef jerky in my cupboards, but Granddaddy had spent a couple of weeks with me last fall, and the stuff doesn't seem to have an expiration date. My sister was supposed to be in charge of The Grands while The Parents were on vacation together.

It's a strange family situation. If this were on a reality show, you'd swear they were making it all up. "The Parents" consist of my mother, Brandy, and my stepfather, Dave, my father, George, and my stepmother, Anne. They live next door to each other in The Meadows, a 55+ golf community. On purpose. As in they bought houses right next to each other because they get along great and hang out together. Yep, I know it's weird, but it gets weirder. They moved to The Meadows because each of The Parents have one parent of their own still living at 80+, aka "The Grands," and things would be easier to manage if everyone was in the same place, right? The reality was that The Parents took multiple vacations every year to get away from The Grands, and my sister and I had to pick up the slack when they were gone.

"How 'bout a beer?" Granddaddy Hacker asked.

"No," I said sharply. "What are you doing here? You're supposed to be in Delaware at The Meadows, and Ashley is taking care of everything for you while The Parents are on vacation."

"Yeah, yeah, quit your jawin'," he waved his hand dismissively and changed the channel.

"Why are you here? And how did you get here?" I asked again with exasperation.

"Hitched."

"What! Do you know how dangerous that is?" Completely unbelievable. It was like talking to a teenager.

He raised a bushy eyebrow. "'Fraid I'll get molested?"

"No," I said through clenched teeth. "I'm afraid you'll get dead and I'll be blamed for it."

"Not my time yet. Got a lot of livin' left in me," he declared.

"Okay, then why aren't you doing your livin' at The Meadows?" I asked.

"I'm not livin' with a thievin' sumabitch!" he growled.

"What did Uncle Grover do this time?" It figures. To save money The Parents had moved Uncle Grover and Granddaddy Hacker into one unit and Mammaw and Aunt Pearl into the other. They couldn't have set up a more dysfunctional arrangement if they'd tried.

"The man is a thief, I told you!" he huffed. "And he's light in the loafers to boot!"

I pinched the bridge of my nose. I heard my cell buzz with a text message, but ignored it. "Uncle Grover had three children, Granddaddy. He's not gay."

"Then why is he always prancing around arranging flowers and burning candles? I can't stand candles!" Granddaddy had worked himself into a lather thinking about the candles. "And that little dog of his! Always yapping, yapping—like some old woman. I can't take it no more!"

Obviously I was going to have to be the reasonable one here. "Okay, I get all that. Uncle Grover is not easy to live with." *Like you are*, I wanted to add, but restrained myself. "But he's not a thief. What do you think he stole?"

"He stole my rifle!"

Now I knew that my stepmother had confiscated Granddaddy's rifle after he and Aunt Pearl tried to set up a target range in the open space at The Meadows. Luckily, my Dad happened to be coming back from Wal-Mart—where he spends an abnormally large part of his day—and was able to disarm the two troublemakers before The Meadows' security guard showed up. Granddaddy, however, didn't know this. He thought it was locked in his rifle case.

"How do you know he stole your rifle?" I asked carefully.

"Because it wasn't in its case," he replied.

"But how did you open the case? Anne kept the key, so there would be no more incidents."

He looked a little sheepish. "I broke the lock. Well, it's my gun, ain't it? Annie got no right to keep a man from his gun. The constitution says so!"

I wasn't getting into a second amendment debate with Granddaddy Hacker, but I think he could be a poster child for the gun control movement. I did some more useless cleansing breathing. "It wasn't Uncle Grover, Granddaddy. It was Anne. She never locked the gun back in the case. She kept it."

His eyes narrowed. His face reddened, sort of like when Yosemite Sam blows his top. "What? I didn't raise my only daughter to treat me this way. Take a man's gun away from him. I'm going to whip her keister for this!"

I sometimes felt the same way about my stepmother, and it would be fun to see Granddaddy try to "whip her keister", but I defended her nonetheless. "She was only trying to make sure you didn't get in trouble. She was doing her job as your daughter. She was protecting you."

"Don't this beat all," he said, shaking his head. "I guess I was wrong about Grover."

I sat down next to him on the couch and patted his arm. "It's okay. As soon as your pants are dry, I'll take you home, and you can patch things up. Maybe you could play Scrabble with him. You know how much he loves Scrabble." I picked up my cell phone. Two texts from my sister.

"No," he said firmly, "I think I'll stay here."

I froze. "What?"

"Let's just say I don't think Grover will be welcomin' me home with open arms." He started flipping through channels again.

"What did you do?" I asked, dread hitting my gut. Only he was saved answering as my phone rang. It was my sister.

"Is Granddaddy there?" she snapped.

"Yes, Ashley. He showed up at my door with no pants on. Great job keeping an eye on The Grands!" I snapped back.

"Well, you can just keep him!" she shouted.

"Whoa—just hold on—he is not staying with me. I had my turn."

"Did he tell you what he did?" she asked.

I glanced over at Granddaddy surfing the channels and looking guilty. "We were just getting to that," I said.

"He took Honey Bunny to the SPCA!"

My eyes narrowed at Granddaddy. "You took Uncle Grover's dog to the SPCA?" I whispered furiously at him.

My sister continued, "And when Uncle Grover found out, he fainted and hit his head. I'm at the hospital with him now."

"Is he okay?"

"I don't know. The doctor is coming in now," she said. "I'll call you back later."

I just sat there staring at my phone for a second.

Granddaddy shifted on the couch. "So, did the old coot go get his stupid mutt from the pound or what?" he asked pretending not to care.

I turned on him. "I don't know, Granddaddy, because Uncle Grover is in the hospital."

He furrowed his brow. "Oh, what the heck! That guy is a pansy. Did he up an' faint again?"

"Yes, he fainted, and he hit his head. As in knocked out! You should be ashamed of yourself," I said shaking my head.

He actually looked like he might be feeling bad. "Maybe leaving the ransom note and the hair was a bad idea," he conceded.

"Ransom note? What hair?" I asked incredulously.

He shrugged. "Well, I left a note saying, 'Give me my gun, and you'll get the mutt back.' I cut off that stupid pony tail on the top of her head, bow an' all, as proof. Just like in the movies," he added. "I thought about bringin' her here with me. But that dog is mean. She bit me twice when I was tryin' to cut her hair off. So I tied her to the front door of the SPCA."

I dropped my head in my hands. I just couldn't take anymore. I needed a drink. Now. I stood up and resolutely walked to my room. I changed into a sweater and jeans and swapped out my heels for suede boots. I checked the mirror. Not bad. I pulled my hair from the confines of a tight pony tail and tucked my long bangs behind one ear. In the kitchen I put Granddaddy's pants into the dryer and pulled some leftover Chinese out of the fridge.

"There's Chinese on the counter. Cover it with a paper towel before you microwave it, please," I said as I grabbed my purse.

"You goin' to McGlynn's?" he asked.

"Yes, and you're not," I said firmly.

"That ain't no way to treat your Granddaddy," he complained.

"You don't have pants," I pointed out. "So you can't go. And, frankly, I need some alone time."

He acknowledged his lack of pants with a shrug. "You singin' tonight?" he asked.

"No. Just drinking," I said as I shut the door behind me.

It was almost 7:00 p.m. when my feet touched the bricks on West Street. The two block walk to McGlynn's was cool and quiet. For a moment I almost forget that I had a crazy, old man with no pants on in my house. Oh, and don't forget dog-napper. I checked my phone, wondering if I should call my sister. We had an on again off again relationship. We got *on* each other's nerves and pissed each other *off,* but were pretty good friends. I caved and called.

"Well, he's alive," she said dramatically. "No thanks to Granddaddy! I just picked up Honey-Bunny and still have to pick up the kids from swim practice."

"I'm bringing Granddaddy home tomorrow after I get off work," I said.

"No way. Uncle Grover is adamant that he isn't living with him anymore," she said.

"Then I'll bring him to your house," I replied.

"Don't you dare!" she shrieked.

"Hey, you're in charge while The Parents are gone," I reminded her. "He stays with you until they get back and work things out."

Total silence on the other end. I had her, and she knew it.

"Great! Just what I need. Let's just make Ashley's life a little more like Hell on Earth," she said. Again with the drama. "While the perfect Diana lives the life of a rock star."

I rolled my eyes. I can't believe I called her. "I temped for a vampire today. I wouldn't call that the life of a rock star."

That threw her off. "An umpire?" she said. "So you're working in Baltimore?"

"No, a vampire. You know, with a cape and everything," I said.

"Very funny," she said. "I'm dealing with a disaster here, and you're making jokes. So typical."

"Hey, he was wearing a cape, and his name was Vann Pyres. Seriously! And I was the one with Granddaddy Hacker—without pants I might add—on my doorstop when I got home today. Not you!" I passed a couple, and they gave me a strange look. I lowered my voice. "Look, I get that this has been a shit day for us both, but let's just get through it. I'll bring Granddaddy to your house tomorrow. Hopefully, The Parents can patch things up when they get home."

"Fine," she conceded, "but next time you're in charge of these nuts. I'm turning my phone off. Don't expect me to drop everything just because you've got a gig or some hot-bodied, young grunge singer you're sweatin' it up with."

"Noted. See you tomorrow. Bye."

For the record, I hadn't sweated it up with anybody in over six months. It's not that I don't have offers, but I have rules. I don't date musicians, men I meet in bars, or men that I work with. Don't even get me started about online dating—not happening. So basically, that just leaves men that my friends set me up with or men that I run into on the street. My sister, along with everyone else in my family, was under the delusion that not only was I a barfly, spending my evenings partying it up on the music scene, but that I also enjoyed the company of a countless number of hot, young groupies. Five years ago when I first moved to Annapolis and started working as a musician, I defended my trade and my honor vehemently. I was not a party girl. I was a working musician, living off the fruits of my craft. Well, now that I'm thirty, no closer to selling a song or landing a recording contract, and living mostly off the fruits of temping, I don't mind them making my life more exciting than it is—it gives me hope. And in some strange, dysfunctional way, it shows me that my family still believes in me.

I rounded the corner at West and Calvert. I could hear the sound of bad karaoke blaring from McGlynn's a half a block away. Damn! I forgot about Karaoke Night. Karaoke was the bane of live musicians eking out a name for themselves in every local bar scene. Why pay a musician if your customers could amuse themselves with a $99 Karaoke machine? Hey, a couple of them might even be good singers, said the bar owners. Yeah, right. I hated karaoke. The martinis better be good and strong tonight.

* * *

"Lady Di," called Woody from behind the bar. Yes, his name was Woody like from *Cheers*. But I'd learned not to mention it. He was a little touchy about it. "Didn't think to see you in tonight. Going to honor us and sing some karaoke?"

I grimaced. Woody knew better. I performed at McGlynn's a couple times a month during the slow season and once a week during the summer. It didn't pay a lot, but it was a short gig, usually nine to twelve and close to home. I had also booked two private parties and a wedding from people who had seen me play here.

"I think I can arrange a drink on the house," he tried to sweeten the offer.

I plopped down in front of him at the bar, my back to the little stage where a woman was crooning a drunken version of "I Will Survive."

"Nope," I said, "not for ten free drinks."

"What you drinking tonight? Appletini?" he asked.

I shook my head. "Make it a plain vodka with two olives."

He whistled. "Wow, you must have had a bad day."

"Granddaddy Hacker showed up at my door today with no pants on."

"'Nough said. I'll make it a double. Hacker is one crazy dude." He went to work making my drink.

"Yes, he is," I agreed. Woody had met Granddaddy last fall. That was when I learned how irritated Woody could get about the whole *Cheers* thing.

Woody set my drink in front of me. It looked heavenly. The screeching in my ears, though, was ruining the moment. "Karaoke sucks," I muttered.

Woody said, "I would've thought you'd be more supportive of your friend. She may not be good, but she's got passion." He pointed to the stage.

I turned around. Sure enough, there was Carol, just launching into a barely intelligible rendition of Dolly Parton's "9 to 5." She was still in her work clothes, and her bob was slightly mussed. Her owl glasses were gone. Right in the middle of belting out the song she said into the microphone, "Diana, is that you?" She squinted blindly into the stage lights. "Yoo-hoo," she called to me and waved.

The small audience turned in unison to look at me.

I waved back.

She covered the mike and mouthed to me, "I'll be right there."

I gave her the thumbs up and turned back towards the bar. I took a big gulp of my martini. Man, what a day!

CHAPTER THREE

It turns out that those first quarter reports Carol had been so worried about were, actually, bad. Really bad. So after making things semi-presentable at the office she headed to McGlynn's to meet me and drown her sorrows in a martini. Of course, I was busy with Granddaddy. So Carol had started without me and kept drinking until karaoke started. Karaoke has the uncanny ability to turn otherwise quiet, respectable people into mike-hogging divas. Its siren call lures even the most timid to belt out songs they will spend weeks trying to erase from their minds. Okay, the liquor might have something to do with it too.

I ordered Carol a glass of ice water and watched her try to stay upright on the bar stool. One of her pumps fell to the floor. The other one dangled precariously from one toe.

"I can't believe this is happening," she slurred. "I love my job. I'm good at my job, you know," she said wagging her finger back in forth in front of my nose.

"You're the best!" I replied brightly. "Mr. Greene is going to be impressed with you." Just not right now so much.

"Did you like my last song?" she asked, changing the subject quickly.

"It was great. I didn't know you liked to sing."

"I didn't know it until now myself," she giggled. "Maybe we can do a duet. That would be fun!"

Woody had been listening to the conversation. "Yeah, Di," he said, "go get the book."

I gave him a back off look that he chose to ignore.

"Oh, pleeease!" begged Carol. "This could be our last chance. I may have to move back to Philly and live with my mother."

Oh, brother. I hated showing up at the party late when everybody was three drinks ahead of me. "Another martini, Woody," I said as I headed to the stage to retrieve the song book.

When I returned with the book a tall, well-built man was leaning on the bar next to my stool. He was ordering a beer from Woody and making small talk. His hair was short and brown and was just starting to get a little shaggy around the edges. The skin on his smooth shaven face was tan. He looked like a man that spent a lot of time outdoors. Maybe out on the water, one of those trust fund yacht guys. Yawn.

I slid into my seat and set the book on the bar top with a thump. Carol pounced, eagerly flipping through the pages looking for just the right song for us to sing. I ignored the Thurston Howell III wannabe.

"How about 'The Night the Lights Went out in Georgia?'" she suggested.

I made a face. I could see that if I didn't find something semi-decent this was going to be a train wreck of epic proportions. "It needs to be something easy to sing that we both know most of the words to," I said.

"I know," she said excitedly pointing her finger at the page. "'The Rose' by Bette Midler!"

"That sounds like a winner," Thurston Howell chimed in over my shoulder.

"See," said Carol, "Mark thinks it's a good choice." Like I was supposed to know who Mark was.

"Well, then maybe *Mark* would like to sing it with you," I suggested turning around to face the interloper.

"Not me," he said with a grin, holding up his hands. "I'm just trying to help you ladies out. Let's start over," he said offering me his hand. "I'm Mark." He had a wide friendly smile, and his hand was warm and a little calloused. Which clashed with my Trust-Fund-Yacht-Guy theory just enough to give me pause.

I shook his hand. "Diana," I said. "And it looks like you already met Carol." We both glanced over at Carol taking another swig from her glass and peering into the song book. Her face was inches from the page. Her glasses were nowhere in sight. She was in her own little buzzed world.

"Yes, she was explaining that you two were going to do a duet next. She sure gets into karaoke," he said and took a sip of his beer. I didn't get the pickup vibe from him. More of the you're-pretty-but-I-don't-need-to-pick-women-up-in-bars vibe. Fine by me, because I didn't date men I met in bars.

"What brings you to Annapolis, Mark?" I asked.

"Hey, how do you know I'm not a local?" he teased.

"Because if you were a local, you'd either have been in here before or would have never set foot in here to begin with. McGlynn's has two kinds of customers—the locals who work for a living and come in looking for a good deal and the tourists. Now you," I said tilting my head and looking up at him, "are neither."

"You're right," he said. "I'm neither. I'm here on business. I'm a commercial real estate developer. I grew up in Virginia, but I live in Atlanta now." As he spoke I couldn't help staring into his bright blue eyes. He smelled wonderful. I leaned in a little to get a better whiff. He was still talking, but I had no idea what he was saying.

I nodded in agreement. He leaned behind me and tapped Carol on her shoulder. "How about 'These Boots are Made for Walking' by Nancy Sinatra? Diana likes it."

Wait a minute! I didn't say that. I knew the song—too well. Aunt Pearl used to make me sing it with her every time I came over to see her. But no way did I say I wanted to sing it now. Argh! He had distracted me with his hypnotic eyes and delicious smell. What was that smell? There was cologne and soap, but also a leather smell mixed with fresh cut grass maybe. It was dizzying. I finished my second martini and gave Woody the one more signal.

"Perfect choice, Diana!" Carol said, pulling on my sleeve. "Let's go write our names down."

"You go ahead. I'll be over when I get my drink," I told her.

Carol trotted off happily. She seemed to be sobering up a little. I guess the water was helping.

Me on the other hand…a fresh martini was facing me when I turned back around. And so was Mark, wearing a big smile. "That was a dirty trick," I said.

"What did I do?" he asked with mock innocence.

"You knew that I was trying to get out of singing with her."

"Yeah, but if you get up there and sing with her, I can stare at you all I want without it being awkward," he said matter-of-factly.

I felt a fluttering in my stomach and a flush spreading below. I met his eyes, because I knew it was a challenge, but I looked away first. I'm no good at flirting.

"Yoo-hoo, Diana," Carol shouted into the microphone. "It's our turn."

Saved by karaoke! (Maybe it wasn't *all* bad after all.) I grabbed my drink and hurried to the stage. I was starting to feel the effects of the two and a quarter martinis. Good. A drink or two was perfect for getting up in front of a crowd and singing. More than that and you forgot the words. That's a lesson most singers learn the hard way. Of course, when you're singing karaoke it doesn't matter how much you've had to drink because the words are right there in front of you. I guess that's why karaoke and bars go so well together.

The music had already started to twang as I climbed on stage with Carol. "Here she is," Carol said like the emcee for a beauty pageant. "Isn't she lovely and tall!" she added looking up at me. I felt like an Amazon next her. I looked down at her stocking feet with reinforced toes. It didn't help that she had left her heels at the bar.

There was a smattering of applause from the small audience, and I could hear Woody's shrill whistle from the bar loud and clear. Must be something they taught in bartender school, I thought randomly. I was feeling nervous. Bizarre. I played out at least a hundred times a year, and I was worried about singing karaoke at McGlynn's? Really? It was all that manly smelling Mark's fault. Just like the big bad wolf. The better to watch you with, my dear. Who says stuff like that?

And then we were singing. I gave it my best shot. We even managed a few Nancy Sinatra dance moves. By the end of the song the crowd was singing along and a couple of people had come up in front of the stage to dance. Not bad. And not once did I look over at Mark. Points for me.

Carol was over the moon. She high-fived me as we were leaving the stage and said, "Next time you play out we should do a couple of songs together. Though, we'd need to practice, of course." Great! I'd created a monster.

I felt like a school girl as I walked with Carol up to the bar where Mark stood clapping his hands. "Great job!" he said with genuine enthusiasm. "You were terrific. You need to take your show on the road."

Carol beamed. "That's just what I told Diana!"

I gave him a dirty look. He smiled mischievously.

The bar was getting busier, and Woody was flying around mixing drinks and pouring beers. "Another martini, Di?" he asked.

I looked at the time—almost nine—and looked at my empty glass. "Better make it ice water," I said.

"No more water for me," Carol declared. "I'm celebrating!"

Woody nodded to me and then stopped and looked over my shoulder at the front door. He made a face. Shaking his head, he said, "You might want to rethink that drink order, Di." He pointed to the door.

Granddaddy Hacker stood in the doorway, thankfully wearing pants. He was carrying my guitar case. "I'll have a Jack on ice," I said as I stood up.

"Hey, Queenie Baby," Granddaddy called across the room. "Thought you might want to buy your Granddaddy a drink and play me some Patsy." He plopped my guitar down next to Mark's bar stool.

"I told you to stay home. I wanted some alone time, remember?" I said between clenched teeth.

Granddaddy looked pointedly at Mark. "Don' look like you havin' too much alone time here."

"That's beside the point," I told him. "Why did you bring my guitar? I'm not playing tonight. I'm drinking."

"You didn't say I couldn't come," he said. "You just said I didn't have no pants to wear. Well now I do! Got 'em out of the dryer myself." He was actually proud of that. Anything domestic he called "woman's work," and he expected someone else to do it for him. This list included, but was not limited to:

doing laundry or dishes, cooking, performing yard work, and doing any form of cleaning. I hadn't yet figured out what, if anything was "man's work."

"That's not the point, and you know it!" I said.

Granddaddy pulled himself onto a stool and banged on the bar top. "Barkeep!" he called.

I groaned.

Woody looked at me and walked over to him. "Good to see you again, Mr. Hacker," he said. "What can I get you?"

Granddaddy cackled. "Well, I'd like me a piece of that brunette over there," he said pointing to Carol, "but I don' think she's on your menu. Hah!" He slapped his palm on the bar top.

Carol glanced down the bar at Granddaddy and took him in with a glance. Nope. She wasn't that drunk.

"Granddaddy, just order a drink. One drink," I said sternly.

"Okey-dokey," he said agreeably. "One drink and a Patsy song."

"Not going to happen tonight."

"Aw," said Mark. "Sing your Granddaddy a Patsy song."

"Listen to the man, Queenie Baby! My days might be numbered. Could be your last chance," he said with a sniff.

"Fat chance," I said to Granddaddy. I turned on Mark. "And you stay out of this."

"Come on Queenie Baby, be a sport," he teased.

"Don't call me that!" I fumed. Granddaddy had been embarrassing me since I was a teenager with that nickname. He used to tell Granny Hacker that she'd better treat him like a king or he'd replace her with a young, sexy Queenie Baby. As much as he threatened, though, Granddaddy never replaced her. In fact, he was still a confirmed bachelor ten years after she'd gone to the big bargain store in the sky. Granddaddy meant it as a term of endearment, instead of something like "Cutie Pie." I mean after all, what woman wouldn't want to be a Queenie Baby?

"It's cute," Mark said with a twinkle in his eye.

I could feel myself blushing. Unbelievable. I had to get laid more often. This was ridiculous. I deliberately ignored his comment and leaned over to take a big swig of Jack. Granddaddy ordered Southern Comfort on the rocks.

"A little SoCo to warm my so cold cockles," he cackled as he downed it in one motion. He slammed his glass down on the bar and called, "Barkeep, another SoCo. And keep 'em coming. If my granddaughter ain't gonna sing for me, then I'm gettin' drunk!" He clinked shot glasses with Carol who was drinking something that looked like cappuccino out of another shot glass. Oh, good grief! This was getting out of hand.

I could see Mark out of the corner of my eye. Arms crossed, leaning against the bar watching my every move. Why did he have to smell so good?

"Fine," I said. "I'll sing. One song and then we're out of here. We've got work tomorrow." I looked pointedly at Carol. She raised her shot glass.

Granddaddy waved his hand in the direction of Greene's. "That ain't nothin'. You're just tempin', and she runs the place." He gestured to Carol. "Who's gonna know if you're a wee bit late."

"We aren't going to be late," I said with determination. "One song and we're gone."

I pulled my guitar out of the case and dug through my pockets for a pick. There was always one in a pocket somewhere. Success!

Mark leaned in close and said, "A girl with a guitar. I don't think there is anything sexier."

I flipped my long blond hair out from under the strap, looked up at him and replied, "You should see me play the guitar naked." I turned around and headed for the stage before he could reply. Take that! I'm not some swooning teenager. No sir, I'm a grown woman who can play the game too.

I was feeling pretty good about myself—and definitely a little tipsy—as I climbed up on stage. I plugged my acoustical guitar into the stage amp and repositioned the microphone. I strummed a few notes to check the sound and said, "I know it's karaoke night, but my crazy Granddaddy is sitting over there at the bar." I pointed to Granddaddy, and the audience (all ten or so) turned around to look. Granddaddy waved to them. "And he's threatening to keep doing shots until I play him a Patsy Cline song." A couple of the rowdier customers hooted in support of Granddaddy and his shots. "So I'm dedicating this song to my crazy Granddaddy, my crazy day, and all my crazy friends." Everyone in the bar clapped and hooted.

As I plucked the melody out on my guitar, the room quieted down, and I began to sing "Crazy." I loved anything by Patsy, but this song was definitely at the top of my list. It just felt sad and romantic, hopeful and hopeless all at once. Transposing it to play on the acoustical guitar had been difficult. But it had been a labor of love. As I sang the last few notes, I looked up and saw Mark with his eyes closed. What the heck! Geez, I'm putting people to sleep with my singing. Not good when you're supposed to be a professional musician. When I strummed the last note there were a few seconds of silence before the room erupted in applause and whistles. There were also a few catcalls, but I think that was Granddaddy.

"Thank you so much," I said into the microphone. "If you enjoyed that, I'll be performing at McGlynn's again this Friday night from nine to twelve. Hope to see you here." I unplugged my guitar and headed back to the bar.

Granddaddy had SoCo shots lined up on the counter. One for each of us. I glanced over at Mark. He looked almost serious. As I was putting my guitar back in its case, he leaned over and said, "You're great. I mean amazing."

"Well, that's good. I was worried I was keeping you awake."

He wrinkled his forehead.

"Your eyes were closed through most of the song," I said, not even trying to mask my exasperation.

He looked like I had caught him with his hand in the cookie jar. "I had to close my eyes, so I could actually listen to you instead of just staring at you."

"Is that supposed to be a compliment?" I joked.

"Yes." Then he took my hand, turned it over, and kissed the palm gently. Warmth spread up my arm and down my body to all the good parts. Wow. What was that?

I had to put a stop to this. Remember the rules, Diana! You met him in a bar. It's a no go. Non-negotiable. I pulled my hand back. "I'm sorry, but I don't date men I meet in bars."

Granddaddy slurred, "Come on you two. A toast." We all raised our shot glasses. "To my Queenie Baby!"

I rolled my eyes and downed it.

Mark leaned closer and smiled wickedly. "Who said anything about dating, Queenie Baby?"

I sucked in my breath, ready to tell him all about himself.

"Whoa, hold on there girl," I heard Granddaddy say. Next thing I knew, Carol was face down on the floor. "Barkeep," he announced loudly, "we have a patron down. I repeat we have a patron down."

Woody gave me a look that said we had worn out our welcome.

"We'll take our check now." This place was my bread and butter. No need to piss off the "barkeep." "Come on Granddaddy. It's time to go." I pulled on his sleeve and ran around him to get Carol.

"Aww, the party was just gettin' started," he complained and looked eagerly for something else to drink.

"I have to play here again Friday. I don't want to lose this gig."

That stopped him. "Yep, you're right," he said with a drunken nod. "Don't shit where you eat. Time to make tracks."

Mark got on the other side of Carol and lifted her to her feet. He propped her against the bar stool as I bent to get her purse. I noticed she was still in her stocking feet. No shoes in sight. Well, it wasn't that far of a walk. I looked up at Mark. "You don't happen to have a car, do you?"

"No. Not that I would drive right now even if I did," he replied shaking his head. "I'll flag down a cab."

"No chance a cab is going to stop for this motley crew. We've got 'backseat barfers' written all over us." I pushed a stray hair out of my eyes. "We'll just have to walk back to my place. It's only two blocks. Carol can stay with me tonight." I sighed. This was going to be fun.

"Need a hand?" he asked. "Or was that an invitation?" He had such a wicked, sexy grin that I swear I almost turned it into one.

"You can just keep your hands to yourself," I said. "And keep your lips off mine!" I turned away to root through my purse for my debit card to pay the bill. I put the card on the bar.

But Woody said, "It's paid," and nodded at Mark who was putting on his coat. Fab.

That just burned me. Did he think he was going to pay for a couple of drinks and follow me home to bed? "Thanks, Woody. Sorry if we were a little rowdy. I'll see you Friday."

"Hey, no problem," he said easily. "Besides, your new boyfriend made it well worth it." Woody turned around and rang the bell over the cash register. A bartender signal that he had just received a good tip.

I looked up at the ceiling and pinched the bridge of my nose. I felt like banging my head on the bar.

"Are you ready?" Mark asked from behind me.

I turned around and he had Carol tucked under one arm and my guitar case in the other hand. "I'll let you get your Granddaddy," he said with a charming smile. "He looks like he might bite."

At this point it was getting late, and I had no other choice. Not that a little part of me (you know the part) didn't like the idea of Mark knowing where I lived. Oh, God, please don't let him be one of those charming serial killers. That's all I needed right now.

CHAPTER FOUR

———

The walk back was relatively uneventful. With the exception of Carol vomiting in the street and Granddaddy peeing behind a Dumpster, all went smoothly. Mark and I barely spoke. The tension was rising the closer we got to my condo. We finally reached the front door.

As I fumbled for my keys, Granddaddy wandered off the sidewalk and into the hedges in front of Mrs. Kester's condo. Before I could stop him, he rapped on the window, yelling, "Come on out and play, you old bitty. I'll take my drawers off, so you can have another look." Granddaddy started to unbuckle his belt. Mrs. Kester's light came on just as I opened the front door.

"Whoa, there Mr. Hacker," Mark said. "You don't want to do that."

He sat my guitar down and leaned Carol against the wall to go after Granddaddy. Granddaddy saw him coming, whipped his pants off, and threw them in Mark's face. Mark made a grab for him, but Granddaddy faked left and ran out into the open area in front of the building. He was impressively agile for a drunken old man. Mark turned to look at me for direction. I shrugged, not sure what to do.

"Get your pants on Granddaddy," I yelled. "And get in this house now! Or you can stay out here tonight."

That stopped him in his tracks.

"You're a party pooper, girl! Don' let an old man have his fun," he complained as he grabbed his pants from Mark. "I was just about to show this feller my old wrasselin' moves."

"His what moves?" Mark asked.

"Wrestling. He used to wrestle in high school," I explained.

"Yep," Granddaddy said proudly. "An' this here move was my specialty." And quick like a jack rabbit, Granddaddy hooked his leg around Mark's leg and put him flat on his back. He leapt on top of Mark and straddled him. "Works every time," said Granddaddy proudly.

I looked down at Mark.

"He doesn't wear underwear, does he?" Mark asked.

"Nope," I said sympathetically.

There was some rustling at the front door. I heard a gasp as Mrs. Kester stepped out onto the porch and took in the scene. "I want you to know that I just called the police," she huffed. "I am reporting you for lewd behavior and drunkenness!"

"Get off him, Granddaddy!" I yelled. "Right now." Granddaddy rolled off Mark with a grumble. "And get your pants on now!"

Mark stood up and dusted himself off.

"Show's over, Mrs. Kester," I said irritably. I'd had enough of this day.

"I'm going to press charges when the police get here. I don't have to live with this kind of riff raff," she yelled shrilly.

Carol suddenly straightened up, walked over to Mrs. Kester and vomited all over her house slippers.

"Help!" Mrs. Kester shrieked. "She upchucked on me. I'm suing all of you." She ran back into her condo and slammed the door. I felt kind of bad for her.

I heard the sound of police sirens in the distance. This couldn't be happening. Granddaddy must have realized what kind of trouble he was in, because he had skulked away up the stairs without a word.

"You know I could have taken him, right?" Mark said. I think he was only half-kidding.

I cocked my head and looked at him. "I'm not so sure about that."

"No way!" He grinned, the humor of the situation was starting to sink in. "Not fair. I demand a rematch."

"Diana," Carol croaked, "I want to lie down."

"Do you mind getting her up the stairs?" I asked.

"No problem. At least my odds of getting barfed on have gone down."

He scooped up Carol, and I grabbed my guitar case. I opened the door and got everyone inside just as the police showed up.

"Probably best if you go down to meet them," Mark said as he laid Carol on the couch. My dog, Max, ran around sniffing everyone with interest. His little fluffy white tail wagged with all the new smells.

"Yeah, great," I said as I made my way downstairs. The police were knocking on Mrs. Kester's door. She opened it, shrieked something, and pointed at me. Wonderful, I thought, the ending of a lovely day. I'm getting arrested.

I waited on the landing for them to finish in her apartment. A few nail-biting minutes passed before the two officers filed out. Before I could say a word, one of the officers looked up and said, "Hey, don't you play guitar on Thursday nights over at The Crab Deck during the summer?"

What was this? A fan? "Yes," I said hesitantly.

"Diana, right?" he asked. I nodded.

"Wow, I never miss a night when you are playing." He pulled off his hat. "I always sit at the end of the bar by the big crab? John Laney."

I actually recognized him. He bought me a margarita whenever I played a Jimmy Buffet song. Great guy. I always expected him to ask me out, but he never did. "I sure do. Small world, huh?"

"Yeah!" he said brightly.

I looked around at the other officers and at Mrs. Kester's door. "So," I began, "I guess my neighbor got a little worked up."

He waved his had dismissively. "Don't worry about it," he said. "She's drunk. We could smell the alcohol on her when she opened the door. I told her she's lucky we didn't fine her for making a false complaint." He smiled. I smiled back. He was quite attractive, in a clean-cut kind of way.

"Okay," I said. "So no harm done?"

"None. We're sorry to disturb you," he said politely. As he started to make his way back to the door, John turned around and said, "Hey, when you playing again? I'd sure like to hear you sing some Jimmy Buffet. Makes me feel like summer's just around the corner."

"I'll be at McGlynn's this Friday, nine to midnight. You should stop by," I said meaning it.

"Will do!" he said and clapped his hands together. "I'm looking forward to it. Practice up on that Jimmy Buffet now."

As I shut the door behind me, I leaned up against it and breathed a sigh of relief. That had been a close one. Poor Mrs. Kester. This was not going to help our neighbor relations. I wearily climbed the stairs and opened my door. Inside, Carol was on the couch snoring noisily from under a blanket. Granddaddy was sprawled out on the recliner next to her. He was also covered by a quilt from my bedroom. Mark sat at the breakfast bar, his long legs stretched out in front of him, sipping a glass of ice water, and munching on beef jerky. Max, my Shih Tzu-Poodle mix, was waiting patiently to claim his share. They both looked over at me at once. I think Max looked irritated to see me. He knew his beef jerky treat was coming to an end.

Mark smiled lazily and said, "If I weren't so beat, I'd walk over there, pick you up and carry you to that comfy looking bed in there."

My stomach flipped. Warmth spread all over. But I gave him the "yeah, right" look and said, "Well, I guess getting pinned by an eighty-two-year-old man can be pretty tiring."

"I'm never going to live that one down, am I?"

I walked towards him. "Nope. Not a chance." I reached down to pat Max on the head. He growled at me. I was getting between him and the beef jerky.

"Bad boy!" I said. "Go to your bed. Go on!"

Max moped off to his bed, turning once to look back at the beef jerky still in Mark's hand. He gave me a dirty look, like if he hadn't been cursed with dog paws he would have given me the finger.

Mark raised his eyebrows. "Boy, he's really devoted to you."

"Normally, he is," I said defensively. "He just has some food aggression issues." I looked at the clock. Oh, my God! It was one in the morning. What a mess!

"Well, I'd better get going. Busy day tomorrow. How about you?" he asked as he put on his coat.

"Well, after I get these two going in the morning," I said indicating Granddaddy and Carol sprawled out and snoring on my furniture, "I have to go back to temping for a vampire."

Mark raised an eyebrow. "What does temping for a vampire involve?"

"I see by your look that you don't believe me."

He gave me a smile.

I continued, "His name is Vann Pyres, and he actually wears a black cape. I have to turn hand-written manuscripts—written with a quill and inkwell, mind you—into formatted Word documents." I cringed just thinking about my day tomorrow.

"Spinning straw into gold, huh?" he asked with a smile. He stepped close enough for me to catch a whiff of him. So intoxicating. "So Carol assigns you to these temp jobs?"

I nodded. "Yep, I've worked for her for three years. She takes good care of me. She does a great job." We started to walk over to the door.

He glanced over at the couch.

"Well," I said hurriedly, "tonight is not a fair representation of her normal professional self. She was just having a bad day. Some quarterly numbers are off, and her boss is coming in tomorrow."

"Sounds tough," Mark said and then reached out and grabbed me around the waist.

His lips were inches from mine and his breath smelled faintly of beef jerky. Spicy, manly—wow—he even made beef jerky smell good.

"I want to thank you," he said softly. "For one of the most interesting nights I've had in a long time." And then his lips were on mine. They were warm and full, and my body flushed in response. I leaned into him and felt the hardness of his lean, tall frame. His tongue traced a lazy outline around my lips, and I was done. I wanted to drag him to the bedroom, but it would just be too awkward with my overnight guests. And I don't date guys I meet in bars. Period. I pulled away first, frustrated and on the edge. Be good, I told myself.

I looked up into his eyes and saw a similar struggle. He leaned back down as if to kiss me again. "My place isn't far from here," he whispered against my lips.

So tempting. "I can't. I have to be here in the morning, and I was serious about what I said before. I don't date, or *sleep* with, guys I meet in bars. And, besides, I just met you." I shook my head. "It's not my style."

Mark pulled himself away and reached for the door knob. "Maybe we can meet somewhere other than a bar," he said hopefully.

"Maybe," I conceded.

"Maybe sooner than you think, Queenie Baby." He leaned forward and kissed my lips lightly.

"I'd like that," I whispered.

"Oh, for the love of Pete, get a room or close the door!" croaked Granddaddy from the recliner.

Mark waved good-bye and mouthed, "Good luck".

I turned around and told Granddaddy to hush up. "Were you listening the whole time?" I asked.

The old coot answered me with a snore.

Ten minutes later I was dressed in comfy pajamas, laying in my comfy bed, wide awake. Thoughts of Mark swirled around in my mind. What if I had said, yes, I'll go back to your place with you? What if I never saw him again? What if this was just some kind of game he plays with women he meets in bars? Sometime around two, I finally fell asleep.

*   *   *

I awoke to screaming. The sun was streaming into my room. It took me a couple of seconds to remember last night. Then it registered in my muddled mind that it was Carol screaming. I jumped up and ran into the living room to find Granddaddy and Max lying comfortably on top of a squirming Carol.

"Get off her," I yelled hitting Granddaddy with a pillow.

"Don' get your panties in a bunch, girl," he said standing up. He was wearing just his shirt again.

"Where are your pants?" I said.

Carol shrieked and peered from under the blankets. It looked like she was still fully dressed.

"I can't sleep with all my clothes on. You know I don' like to wear pajamas. I left my shirt on to be gentlemanly," he explained.

"What were you doing on the couch?" I asked.

"That recliner was killin' my back, so I just squished in next to your friend over there."

I glanced over at a confused looking Carol. Max was lying on her chest growling every time she tried to move.

"You too!" I said as I swatted Max. Max growled. I hit him again. He got the point and stalked off to his food bowl where, of course, there was no food yet. He looked at me like he couldn't believe how bad his luck was that I was the one that picked him out at the SPCA. Right back at you buddy.

"What time is it?" Carol asked, sitting up.

"Seven forty-five," I replied.

"Oh, my God. I've got to get to work. I have to open at 8:30!" She searched around for her purse and found her glasses. "Can I use your bathroom?" she asked.

"Of course, use whatever you need. Is there anything else I can do to help you out?"

"Call me a cab, and, if you could, find a spare toothbrush and a pair of hose." She was already in efficient Carol mode. "Oh," she added as she went into the bathroom, "do you have some pain reliever? I have a killer headache."

Fifteen minutes later Carol was looking more like her old self. Her hair was smooth, her glasses on, and her clothes were a little less wrinkled from the shower steam. Amazing transformation, all things considered. I looked out the window just as the cab was pulling up. "Cab's here," I said.

"My shoes," she said in a panic. "Where are my shoes?"

I looked down. "They didn't make it out of the bar with us. I am so sorry. You can borrow a pair of mine. What size do you wear?" I asked.

"Six," she said looking down at my gigantic feet. "You're what, a ten or so?"

"Nine and a half. Maybe you could stop at a store on the way?" I said hopefully.

"There's no store between here and the office that sells shoes at 8:00 a.m.," she said dejectedly. "I have to go now."

We settled on a pair of my slide on mules that at least she was able to hold on her feet with her toes. As I opened the door to see her out, I almost tripped over a pair of shoes in the doorway. Carol's shoes! It must have been Mark. Carol jumped up and down and kicked off my mules.

"Hey, your new boyfriend is a lifesaver. You keep a hold of that one!" she said and waved goodbye.

An hour later I was dressed in a casual pair of slacks and a bright blue cashmere sweater. I had thirty minutes before I needed to head over to Vann Pyres' hotel, so I decided to hit up Shacks to get Carol a much needed piece of monkey bread and a cup of coffee. She was already knee deep in temporaries by the time I made it to Greene's.

"No. The man told us to unload the truck, and that's what we did," insisted a tall, burly guy with a bald head and tattoos on his neck.

"Mr. Evans," Carol said calmly, "the supervisor said that you and your crew did unload a truck; however, the truck had just been loaded and was en route to a customer for delivery when they realized the mistake. How do think the customer would have reacted upon receiving an empty truck?"

"Hey." He shrugged. "That ain't my problem, lady. We did the job like they asked. I don't get why they fired us." A couple of guys behind him agreed loudly.

This looked interesting.

Carol saw me at the door with her beloved monkey bread and coffee and acted quickly.

"Mr. Evans, I have a job over in Crofton for the rest of the week. The last crew quit because the work was too hard for them," she said, with a challenging look. "Is your crew tough enough or should I get someone else?"

Not five minutes ago Mr. Evans was ready to have a good argument with Carol, then go drinking for the rest of the afternoon, and sometime much later tonight go home and tell his wife how he was unjustly fired. But as much as he couldn't wait to get that first taste of PBR in his mouth, he couldn't admit to being a wuss.

"Oh, my crew can do it," he said firmly. "Yes, ma'am."

Carol jotted down the address. "Okay, do me proud Mr. Evans," she said, as Mr. Evans walked away, the look on his face saying he wondered what had just happened. One minute he was on his way to the bar, and the next he was headed to Crofton to do some job someone else didn't want.

There was silence as the last of the work boots trudged out the door. I handed Carol her coffee and monkey bread. "Maybe this will pick you up," I said with a smile.

Carol took off her glasses and rubbed her bloodshot eyes. "I'm not sure if anything will help, but it can't hurt." She took a big bite of bread just as the phone rang. I ran around the desk and grabbed it for her. "Greene's Staffing Services how may I help you? Mr. Greene? Um, he's not here right now. Can I take a message?" I looked over at Carol in alarm. "Yes, well, we expect him in later today. Okay, I'll give him the message." I hung up the phone and handed Carol the message for Mr. Greene to call someone named David back.

"Oh, God," she said shaking her head. "I guess this means he's coming. I was praying it was all a bad dream from last night."

"So you haven't heard from him since he called yesterday?"

"No. Although he sent me an email right before I closed yesterday telling me he'd be here at 9:30."

I looked up at the clock. 9:33. "Maybe he changed his mind?" I offered.

"Or maybe the spreadsheets I forwarded with figures for the last two quarters to gave him a heart attack."

I scrunched up my forehead. "What is so wrong with the numbers? It seems like you've been pretty busy."

"Oh, the overall sales are fine, but they don't match the receivables. We should have way more cash than we do," she replied.

I frowned. "You mean someone has been stealing from us?"

Carol's face went a shade paler. "I don't know. All I know is the money is missing.

"So who has access to it?" I asked.

"The accountant, old Mr. Greene, and I guess young Mr. Greene." She paused. "And me."

"Maybe the accountant is doing some funny business?"

"I don't know. All I know is that it doesn't look good," she moaned.

The front door creaked open. A tall, handsome man in an impeccably tailored suit walked in and removed his sunglasses. "Carol, I see you found your shoes," he said with a smile.

Carol looked down at her shoes and then up at Mark in horror. "Mr. Greene?" she croaked.

"Yep," he said and turned to me. "Hey, this isn't a bar now is it, Queenie Baby?"

CHAPTER FIVE

———

I was speechless for about ten seconds. Mark was Young Mr. Greene. I had to let that sink in. Oh, poor Carol!

"You knew who we were all along!" I said pointing a finger at him.

"Not all along," he said. "But, yeah, pretty early in the evening."

I glanced over at Carol. She had turned ghostly white. She started to say something…and then fell backwards in a dead faint. I gasped and rushed behind the counter with Mark close behind. I cradled her head in my lap and patted her cheeks.

"You are the most conniving asshole I have ever met!" I said angrily. "Look what you've done!"

He looked surprised. "Me? She was drunk last night. Don't you think that has more to do with her fainting than me?"

I narrowed my eyes at him. "No, I don't. I think you deliberately dropped in here just to freak her out." I paused to take a deep breath and sucked in some eau de Mark in the process. Oh, why did he have to smell so good? "You think she's somehow responsible for your messed up numbers. But she isn't. She's the only reason this place runs as efficiently as it does. What are you just standing around for? Get a wet towel!" I ordered.

He must have been feeling a little guilty because he rushed off to the bathroom.

"Is he gone yet?" Carol asked and opened one eye.

I looked down, surprised to see her staring up at me. Her color was much better. "Yes," I replied, "how long have you been awake?"

"I never actually fainted," she said. "I started to see black around the edges and then I had this sudden idea to fake faint."

I think Carol was a little delirious. "So what now?" I asked.

Carol looked unsure. "I don't know. My plan didn't include what happens after I faint."

"Not much of a plan."

"Yeah," she said sitting up, "but it was all I had at the moment."

Mark came back with a pile of wet paper towels. He looked relieved to see Carol sitting up. Maybe the fainting plan had been a good idea. He handed me the towels, and I made a big show of patting Carol's forehead and telling her to take deep breaths.

"There's a man in the restroom taking a bath in the sink," Mark said. "Should I call someone?"

"No, that's Simon," Carol said. "He bathes here on Tuesdays and Thursdays." She grabbed for the desktop to steady herself. Mark jumped behind her to help her. She winced as she stood up, and it didn't look like she was faking.

"Do I want to know why?" Mark asked, helping her into a chair.

Carol smoothed her jacket. "Because he lives in a shed and doesn't have running water."

Mark stared at her like she was speaking in tongue. "That doesn't explain why he comes here to bathe," he reasoned.

"He comes here," said Carol patiently, "because he works at Harris Manufacturing, and they like him. However, he smelled so bad they were going to terminate him. I offered to speak to him about his hygiene. My HR contact said if I could take care of the smell, then they would keep him." She looked Mark directly in the eyes. "So, as that is one of our biggest light industrial accounts, he bathes here on Tuesdays and Thursdays. Simon is clean, the customer is happy, and we get paid."

Mark shook his head as if to clear it. "Interesting," was all he said.

The phone rang. Carol leaned across the desk to reach for it and winced again. "Ouch!" she exclaimed. "I think something is wrong with my back."

Mark walked around her and answered the phone. "Greene's Staffing Services," he said glancing at Carol. "She's not available at the moment."

I took the opportunity to whisper to Carol. "Is this part of the plan?"

"No," she said, "I think I pulled a muscle in my back when I fell. It's killing me."

Mark seemed to be having trouble on the phone. "Just a second," he said and placed his hand over the receiver. "It's Shaquan Davis, and she says that her baby's daddy took her car this morning, and she doesn't have a way to get to work until eleven."

Carol extended her hand to Mark and he gave her the phone. "Shaquan, it's Carol. Do you want this job or not?" she asked sternly. "Your baby's daddy is BCDC until next year at least. Can you get there in the next fifteen minutes or should I call someone who can?" She paused, listening to the answer. "Okay, have a great day." She handed Mark back the phone.

He looked a little uncomfortable.

"If they hear a new voice, they think they can get one over on you," I explained. I had learned this the hard way a couple of times when I first helped Carol out in the office.

"She was really convincing," he said defensively.

"Yes," Carol agreed, "they always are."

I looked up at the clock. It was 9:40. "I've got to go," I said. "Carol, I'll call you later today." As I walked to the front door I could feel Mark's eyes on me.

"Wait up, Diana," he called.

I kept moving. I had reached the sidewalk when he caught me. He touched my elbow. "I want to apologize," he began. "I never meant for this to happen. I didn't know you would be at the office this morning."

"But you knew last night who we were and never said a word," I pointed out, walking towards my car.

"You're right," he said following me. "I didn't handle it well. I should have said something." He was making it hard to stay mad at him. I had to get away from his hypnotizing eyes and delicious smell.

"I have to go," I insisted as we reached my car. "You're going to make me late for work. I don't think my boss would appreciate it. I've heard he's kind of a dick," I added as I opened my car door.

I started my engine and pulled away, leaving Mark standing on the curb.

*　*　*

I knocked at The Count's door at precisely 10:00 a.m. He answered it immediately like he had either been standing at the door waiting for me to knock or had flown across the room like a bat. In either case, it was a little unnerving.

"Ms. Hudson," he said warmly as he ushered me in. "So glad you enjoyed your work yesterday enough to return." He chuckled. He was sporting a red cape today. Maybe it was his Superman look.

I smiled back. "Was there any doubt?"

"Well, it has proved difficult in the past to keep a temporary more than a few days." He shook his head and took a seat at his desk. "But I'm not sure why."

Now there's a mystery, I said to myself as I sat down in front of him.

"It's been so difficult to find good help," he continued, "that the last few times I've been in town, Miss Smith has assisted me with the manuscripts herself."

Imagine that. Carol had been Vann Pyres' assistant the last couple of times he had been in town. If she wasn't so beat up by life right now, I'd be tempted to take a jab at her myself.

"First, let me say that your work is marvelous, and so speedy, I might add." He smiled encouragingly. "I think this is going to work out beautifully. Second, I would be honored if you would accompany me to lunch this afternoon at 1:00. I would like to celebrate our successful partnership and discuss a couple of other projects that I have on the horizon."

Lunch, really? Lunch with a man wearing a red cape. "How could I refuse?" I asked with a smile.

"Wonderful," he said. "I will call for you at 1:00, and we will dine in the hotel restaurant." He handed me another stack of illegible, hand-written pages and rose to walk me to the door.

An hour and two cups of coffee later, I had finished three pages. I was glad he appreciated my work and might have other projects, because the money sure was good. But lunch? Argh! This day was going downhill almost as fast as yesterday had.

My thoughts turned to last night. Man, why did Mark have to turn out to be such a jerk. If he had just said who he was at the bar, then maybe…maybe what, I asked myself sternly, maybe it would have worked out? No. He would have had two strikes against him. I met him in a bar, and I worked for him. No way this was ever going to be more than a sweet smelling dream.

My phone rang. It was my condo. Oh, God, what now.

"Yes, Granddaddy," I answered.

"I'm hungry, and we're all out of jerky," he complained.

"So find something else to eat. I'm working."

"Guess I could head out and see what I can find," he said.

"Don't you dare open that door," I whispered furiously. "You promised that you would stay put until I got home to take you to Ashley's."

"That's when I thought you had jerky," he said stubbornly. "That man you had over last night musta' ate it all up."

"He was helping me get you two home," I reminded him. "Now make yourself a sandwich or something, and I'll be home at 4:15." I could hear him grumbling as I hung up the phone.

1:00 p.m. rolled around, and I was actually getting hungry. The hotel restaurant was close to the guest office space. At least we weren't leaving the building. That definitely cut down on the chance of running into someone I knew while out with The Count. He arrived crisply at one, red satin cape flapping jauntily as he stopped at the doorway. With a look of distaste he said, "Diana, I can't abide to be in the presence of those things." He pointed at my computer. "I'm sure they will irradiate me with their poisonous electromagnetic fields." Would it make that much difference? I wondered, as I saved my document and went to meet him at the door. Apparently, it was okay if *I* got irradiated by electromagnetic fields.

Evidently he had been to the hotel restaurant before, because no one seemed to notice his red cape. Not even when he flipped it out like a classical pianist sitting down at his instrument when we took our seats. He called the waiter by name. "Phillip, the lady and I will have the chef's vegan lunch special," he said handing both our menus back to Phillip. I looked up at Phillip for a little sympathy. Phillip was busy scribbling on his pad.

"And to drink?" the server without looking up.

"Your best bottle of Chardonnay, of course," said Mr. Pyres.

Well, I wasn't happy with the food choice, but at least there was wine.

"I don't mean to be rude, Diana," he said apologetically, "but I am particular about food. I can't abide to see animal products consumed. So primal," he added, making an ick face.

"Didn't they eat meat in medieval times," I asked.

"Well, of course they did," he said as if he were talking to a child. "Their barbers were also their surgeons, but I doubt you would go to your hairdresser to get your appendix removed." He smiled at his wittiness. I wasn't impressed. I could have done without vegan lunch with The Count. Where's the wine already?

Phillip arrived and opened the wine with a flare. The Count sniffed the cork appreciatively. "Nice," he proclaimed, and swirled a little around in his glass.

Come on and drink already. I was getting antsy. This lunch was taking way too long. I had more medieval drivel to translate and a crotchety old man to drive back to Delaware. I looked at my watch.

"Here you are, my dear." Mr. Pyres handed me a glass of wine. I took a big swig. It was delicious. Finally, something going my way today. I think he was disappointed that I didn't let it breath and swirl it around on my tongue. "It's a fine Chardonnay not a beer, Diana."

"Wonderful," I pronounced. "Thank you for taking me to lunch. You mentioned some additional projects?" The wine was already starting to work its magic. I felt relaxed and ready to handle whatever wacky proposal The Count threw at me.

"Yes," he said. "I would like to engage your services after I leave the area. I will be traveling to do more research. I would like to mail you my manuscript pages as I write and have you submit the finished product directly to my publisher."

Nothing crazy about that. "Sounds great. That would be fine with me." I took another sip of wine. Wow, it was good.

"Good," he said. "Now that we have that taken care of, I have a more personal proposal to discuss."

Oh, here we go, I thought. I knew it was going too well.

Phillip arrived with our vegan lunches. I leaned back to let him place my plate in front of me. I looked down. Not bad. Some fruit and vegetables and flat, cracker-like bread. Vann Pyres tucked in his napkin and made quick work of his plate. I picked at my plate and drank more wine, waiting for him to continue.

"As I was saying, I have need of your services for a more personal matter." He wiped his mouth and continued. "I have spent most of my life traveling the world and researching medieval literature. I'm going to be sixty years old soon and have yet to settle down, I'm sad to say." He looked like a lost puppy. "This year I have resolved to put time and effort into finding that someone special. Then miracle of miracles you appear at my doorstep," he said with a smile.

Whoa, where's this going? He better not be thinking of settling down with me. Geez, you type a few pages correctly, and all of a sudden he's talking about settling down? I needed to put the brakes on this pronto. "Mr. Pyres, I am flattered that you see me as a miracle that appeared on your doorstep, but I don't see how I can help you with settling down."

He held up a hand. "Ahh, but I do," he said with a slightly creepy smile. "I'd like you to help me meet appropriate partners using a *computer*."

What the heck? "You want me to help you meet women online?" I asked incredulously.

He nodded. "You see how desperate I am. I am willing to do anything. Even use one of those infernal devices," he spat out. "I abhor them, but I understand they might be useful to someone in my unique position. If you agree to help me, I will pay you double your hourly rate."

I took another drink of wine. Double pay sounded great, but how impossible of a job would this be? "Just to clarify," I said, "you want to pay me to help you meet women over the internet in hopes of finding someone to live happily ever after with?"

"Exactly what I am proposing." He took another bite of salad.

"Okay," I said slowly, "you realize this means you have to have an online presence, as in email and Facebook accounts? I'll also have to sign you up at dating websites. All kinds of stuff. You sure you want to do this?"

"As long as I don't have to touch one of those things, yes. I would like you to handle all the arrangements on the computer."

Phillip stopped by to see if there was anything we needed and left the check. I took the moment to gulp more wine and consider my career options.

"So are you up for the challenge, Diana?" The Count asked.

It would rate as the most bizarre temporary assignment to date, but for double pay I was in. "Sure thing. When would you like to start?"

*   *   *

I was back in my car and heading for my condo at the stroke of 4:00. I needed to get Granddaddy back to Delaware before he had a chance to cause any more problems. Mr. Pyres and I had agreed to start finding his soul mate tomorrow. I decided to check in with Carol to see how her day went and tell her about my new project. Okay, yes, I was also hoping to hear more about Mark.

I plugged in my Bluetooth and said, "Call Greene's Staffing."

After two rings, a deep male voice answered, "Greene's Staffing Services." Mark! I quickly disconnected the call.

"Call Carol cell," I said.

"Calling Carol cell," the phone assistant answered.

Carol picked up on the first ring. "Hi, Diana," she groaned.

"Hey, what's going on? I just called the office and Mark answered."

"I'm home with a pulled muscle in my back," she said. "He ended up calling a cab to take me to my doctor. I'm on some great pain killers right now, and I'm out of work for the rest of the week."

"Oh man, I'm sorry, Carol."

"No worries at the moment at least. I feel too relaxed to worry right now." She sounded high as a kite. "I think it's kind of funny that Mr. Greene is stuck running his own business. Good luck!" she said with a cackle.

I had to admit that was a pretty funny picture. "I almost feel sorry for him."

"I don't," she sounded miffed. "He confronted me about the cash discrepancies in our first quarter reports. I think he actually believes I might be a thief! Like I'm cooking the books or taking kickbacks or something."

I bit my lip. The way he'd found Carol's business tactics "interesting" that morning I too was worried he might think so. "Don't worry, we'll find some way to set him straight," I promised. Even if I wasn't sure what that was yet.

"Thanks, Diana," she said with a sniff. "How was your day with Mr. Pyres?"

"He took me to lunch."

"Vegan lunch?"

"Yep. And he wants me to work on a special project paying double."

"That sounds promising. What's he want you to do?" she asked.

"Find him a soul mate online," I replied.

"Good one, Diana," she replied sleepily. "You had me going for a minute there."

"I'll give you the details when you're less loopy," I told her.

We hung up just as I pulled up to my condo. No sign of police officers, firemen, or paramedics. That was a start. Mrs. Kester's condo looked dark and deserted. I crept past quietly. In the hallway I detected an odor that smelled suspiciously like fried bacon. I opened my door and found Granddaddy happily munching on a sandwich. Max was sitting on the couch next to him eating a piece of bacon. My kitchen was trashed, but everything appeared to be intact.

"Hey, there Queenie Baby!" he said. "Join us for a bacon and cheese sandwich." He patted the couch. Max looked at me and growled. He knew his bacon and couch moments were numbered.

"No thanks," I said and shooed Max off the couch. "I need to take him for a walk before we head to Ashley's."

Granddaddy nodded in agreement. "I talked to your sister a while ago. She said to tell you Dan's grillin' tonight so yer welcome to stay to dinner. They got his friends over workin' on her screened-in porch this afternoon."

"We'll see," I said as I went off to change out of my work clothes. Dinner at my sister's was not for the faint of heart. Three kids, a psychotic dog, and a redneck husband made for an interesting time on a regular day. Add a bunch of Budweiser drinking, tobacco chewing construction workers, and who knew what could happen.

CHAPTER SIX

——

The ride to Delaware was thankfully uneventful. Granddaddy was more quiet than usual, probably in anticipation of my sister's wrath at his latest antics. The view from the Chesapeake Bay Bridge was particularly beautiful in the late afternoon. We were a little ahead of the five o'clock rush hour, so the trip to my sister's house west of Dover went smoothly. As the scenery sped by, my thoughts turned again to Mark and the missing money. Would he really think Carol was involved? I wondered how he was holding up at the staffing agency without her. I'd bet that was something to see. My phone rang. I clipped on my Bluetooth and answered. "Hello?"

"Diana?"

"Yes?"

"This is Mark at Greene's Staffing."

My stomach fluttered. How did he do that to me? "Yes?" I said again.

"Look," he said, "I know you're not happy with me, but I need your help." He sounded sincere enough.

"With what?" I asked.

Granddaddy leaned over. "If that's yer sister tell her I want some deer tenderloin on the grill."

I tried to cover the headset. "It's not Ashley."

"Who is it then?" he asked.

I waved my hand at him to hush.

"I'm sorry, Mark. You were saying?"

Granddaddy cackled to himself, "Jes' what I thought!"

"Shhh! No, I wasn't speaking to you. I'm talking to Granddaddy," I said.

"You sure spend a lot of time with your Granddaddy," Mark said.

"I'm driving him home to Delaware right now."

"I know it's asking a lot, but since Carol is out with her back the rest of the week she suggested I call you to see if you could fill in during the mornings before you go to your assignment." He sounded desperate. I'm pretty sure I heard cussing in the background.

As fun as it would be to think of him squirming with the temps, he was my boss. "I'll be there tomorrow at 8:00 a.m., but I have to leave by 9:45 to be on time for Mr. Pyres."

"Great! I'll see you then. Thanks, Diana." He sounded relieved.

Me? I wasn't so sure. Did I want to see him again? Definitely. Did I have a plan to convince him that Carol was not his thief? No way.

We pulled up into my sister's long gravel driveway. I think her husband put their double-wide far back from the road so that he would have a reason to buy a snow plow attachment for his pickup. Dirt and dust coated my car as we bounced towards her house. Kids and animals began emerging from the backyard at the sound of our arrival. A variety of work trucks were parked haphazardly next to the house. I pulled up alongside one with an NRA sticker on the window and a bumper sticker that read, "My coon hound is smarter than your honor roll student."

My niece Tiffany and my two nephews, Jason and Josh, came running up as we got out of the car. "Aunty Di," said five-year-old Tiffany, "are you staying for dinner?"

"I'm not sure," I replied bending down for a hug.

"Mommy put chicken out for the grill just in case you are," she said. Well, good to know I wouldn't be forced to eat deer meat. Yuck!

"Yeah," chimed in the older boy, Jason. "Dad says you're too snobby to eat deer meat."

I hugged him. "Not true," I replied. "I just don't like it much." Did I mention my brother-in-law was a complete jerk? Picture Cousin Eddie from the Chevy Chase Vacation movie series meets the Marlboro Man. Definitely not my type.

My sister came out from the back door near the kitchen. "I ought to take a stick to you old man!" she said shaking her finger at Granddaddy.

"I tol' you on the phone don' be takin' me to task," Granddaddy bristled. "It was Annie's fault for takin' my gun without tellin' me."

"Fine," said my sister with her hands on her hips. "I'll leave you to Anne when she gets home next week." She walked over and hugged me, smelling like French fries and Jean Nate. My sister was a head shorter than I and definitely rounder after three kids, but we shared the same long blond hair and blue eyes.

"Stay for dinner," she said. "I thawed some chicken for you."

"I know. Tiffany told me."

"I bet I know something that you don't know," she said slyly.

"What?"

"It's not what, it's who," she said. "Guess who's here for dinner?"

I rolled my eyes. Really? We were playing a guessing game now? She spent way too much time alone with children. "I don't know, Ashley, who?"

"Rick!" she gushed. "He's the one putting on our porch."

"Rick who?" I asked.

"As in Rick your old boyfriend," she said smugly.

"Are you crazy?" I sputtered. Unbelievable. Just what I needed—my sister trying to fix me up with my high school boyfriend.

"I'm leaving," I said and turned around towards the car.

"Hope you're not leaving on my account," called a deep voice from across the lawn.

I flipped around. There he was. Mr. Homecoming himself, Rick Ellis. He was standing next to my brother-in-law, Dan, who was guffawing into his can of Budweiser. Idiot. A couple other construction guys were behind him drinking out of red Solo cups, not sure what to make of the reunion. They were playing a game of Corn Hole. There were groans as one guy's beanbag slid precariously close to the hole.

"Come on over and join us for a game, Sis," said my brother-in-law.

Great, I have to talk to him, or I'm going to look like a chicken.

"Look out boys," he said as I walked over. "Sis, here, has the Lady Luck!"

Ignoring The Idiot, I crossed the lawn to face my past. "Hi, Rick." He was still tall, dark, and handsome, with lines just starting to show around his brown eyes and full-lipped mouth. "Good to see you," I said and held out my hand.

He looked at my hand. "A handshake after twelve years?" he said with a grin. "I don't think so, Diana." He leaned down and wrapped his arms around me. His shirt smelled like sweat and wood shavings. His once lean, athletic frame had filled out with work-hardened muscles.

I pulled away and looked up at him. "Looks like life's been good to you, Queenie Baby," he said with an appreciative glance. "Are you a rock star yet?"

"Thanks," I said flustered by the rush of nostalgia that flooded through me. "Ah, no, not yet. Still working on it." Our eyes locked.

"Stay for dinner," he said. "Let's catch up and see what happens."

Still trying to tell me what to do, I thought. "Not sure about dinner, but I'll take a beer." I looked away first. My brother-in-law jumped into action and dug around in the red cooler full of ice and beer.

He handed me a Coors Lite. "See, I got some of the good stuff just for you, Sis. Go ahead and take my turn," he said pointing to the game and spitting some chew on the ground. He gave me a smile. There were bits of tobacco stuck to his front teeth. His lower lip was protruding slightly. He still had the athletic farm boy physique, but between the beer and my sister's cooking he was starting to get a gut.

My sister and Dan had gotten married right after high school and started having kids a couple of years later. Dan had a decent job with benefits as an HVAC technician for the City of Dover. He loved hunting, ATVs, beer, and my sister. He liked to tease me about being prissy, which I'm not, but he couldn't resist waving deer meat at me whenever I came over for dinner.

"I'm not really up for Corn Hole after the day I've had, Dan," I said.

"Don't blame you. Heard that Granddaddy showed most of Annapolis his whatnots last night," he laughed.

For all his redneck idiosyncrasies he had an infectious laugh. I smiled. "He tried to."

He shook his head. "Can't wait 'til I'm that old," he said loudly and spit again. "I'm going to wave my whatnots anywhere I want." His construction buddies howled. My sister made a face. I didn't want to think about Dan's whatnots waving anywhere.

I opened my beer and took a sip. Yep—just like I remembered. I would definitely be switching to water soon. I'd had enough alcohol in the last twenty-four hours to get me on a rehab reality show. I turned to Rick. "So how's life been treating you?"

"Well enough, I suppose. Doing better now," he added suggestively.

Was my high school boyfriend actually making a play for me now? And, more importantly, why am I liking it? I needed to get away from his hard body and chiseled good looks for a minute. "I'm going to see if Ashley needs some help."

He shrugged. "I'll be here when you get back."

I hurried off towards the house, picking my way through the screen porch construction to the back door. My sister's big stupid yellow Lab, Sally, saw me coming and busted through the screen door. Two giant paws connected with my chest and sent me backwards down the stairs. I fell with a thud onto the bare wood floor. Sally licked my face and slobbered on me. I could hear my brother-in-law guffawing in the background. Great.

Granddaddy's head appeared through the broken screen door. "Stop foolin' with that idiot dog and get in here. Yer sister needs help, and I'm hungry."

As I pushed Sally off of me, Rick appeared at my side. "You okay?" he asked, helping me up.

"Just fine," I replied wiping dog drool off my shirt.

He laughed. "Some things never change. Remember that time we were at Brian's party and you walked into the sliding glass door. How many stitches did you get?"

"The dog knocked me down!" I said testily. "I'm not as clumsy as I used to be. I get up on stage on a regular basis, you know."

He gave me a smoky look. "That just got my imagination revved up."

"Well, rev it down!" I said and stomped up the stairs.

It looked like a toy factory had just exploded in the middle of my sister's living room. Sponge Bob blared loudly on the over-sized television. Her country chic decor was a mixture of wood and Wal-Mart. Wooden shelves with heart-shaped cut outs loaded with country knickknacks adorned the pink and blue striped walls. Ruffled pastel blue curtains covered the windows. Two deer heads were mounted on either side of television. One of the deer's eyes was crossed. Granddaddy sat on the overstuffed sectional with built-in recliners and wooden flip-down tables, happily munching on a big piece of jerky.

The large, eat-in kitchen was almost organized by comparison. Unfortunately, the theme for this room was teddy bears. A teddy bear border ran the length of the kitchen, teddy bear pictures hung on every square inch of wall space, and teddy bear figurines littered the windowsill.

My sister looked up when I came in. "Can you hand me some salt?"

"Sure," I said, reaching for a salt shaker shaped like—you guessed it—a teddy bear.

"So how's it going with Rick," she asked with a coy smile.

I looked over her shoulder into the bowl. "What's that?" I asked changing the subject.

"Potato salad. And stop changing the subject." She looked up at me. "What happened to you?" she asked taking in my muddy shirt.

"Sally knocked me down."

She rolled her eyes and shook her head. "I swear I don't know how you get from point A to point B without falling down. Wash your hands and help me get finished up."

"Your dog attacked me," I insisted scrubbing my hands. "I didn't trip." Sally decided to trot up to me just at that moment and look up at me with big sad puppy dog eyes.

My sister and I looked down at her. "Yeah sure," my sister said. "That dog attacked you. She's scared of everything."

I gave Sally's head a pat. She was cute. She cowered and peed all over the floor. My sister gave me an evil look and handed me a bunch of paper towels. "Why did you pet her? You know she can't control herself."

Geez! "Why can't you have a normal dog that doesn't pee every time someone looks at it?" Sally wagged her tail. She was happy to be the topic of conversation.

"Oh," my sister said sarcastically, "and your dog is the epitome of self-control."

"Well, he doesn't pee all over everything!"

"Yeah, he's just vindictive, and he bites!"

"Maybe a little vindictive," I agreed, "but definitely not a biter."

"He bit me!" she cried.

"Yeah, but you deserved it. You tried to take food away from him."

My sister gave me an exasperated look. "Uh, my food, remember?"

"That he took because you forgot to give him a goodie after he went outside." It was all quite reasonable.

"Argh!" my sister cried in frustration.

"Maybe we should just agree to disagree," I suggested. She threw a spoonful of potato salad at me. I ducked, and it splattered against the wall. She nailed a smiling teddy bear right between the eyes.

"Mommy!" yelled Tiffany imperiously from the doorway. "We don't throw food."

My sister paused in mid-throw and looked over at our audience of children. "You're right, Tiff," she said regaining control. "Aunt Diana and I were just having some fun."

"Sounded like you two were fightin'," said Jason, ever observant. I shooed the kids back into the living room and then turned back to the sink to wash my hands again.

"You so get on my last nerve," my sister whispered.

"Ditto!" I whispered back. "And why are you trying to fix me up with my old boyfriend? It didn't work then, and it isn't going to work now."

She turned to me and said, "It didn't work then because you didn't try to make it work. Rick is a great guy, and you never gave him a fair chance."

"He didn't want me to go to college. He didn't want me to sing. All he wanted was for me to support him while he did what he wanted to do with his life. He never gave me a chance." It was all true. Rick had been controlling in high school. He had his life planned out and expected me to lockstep with him. Sure, he cared about me, and in many ways he built his life around me, but he never asked me what I wanted out of life.

I looked at my sister, but she wasn't looking at me. I spun around. Rick was standing in the kitchen doorway. "I never knew you felt that way," he said quietly. "You never said anything."

"I guess I didn't know how at eighteen," I said. "I'm sorry."

"Me too," he said and walked away.

There was always drama at my sister's. Always. "Thanks so much, Ashley," I said.

"Hey, don't blame me. You're the one with all the unresolved issues." She picked up a handful of paper plates, plastic utensils, and napkins and shoved them at me. "Time to eat," she said brightly.

*   *   *

Dinner consisted of barbecued deer tenderloin with a few pieces of chicken for the not so adventurous (meaning me), potato salad, pretzel salad, coleslaw, baked beans, and an assortment of chips. Not going to win a healthy eating award, but good nonetheless. The sun was starting to fade, and the temperature had dropped, but it was still pleasant to sit outside at the picnic tables. Made it feel like summer was just around the corner. I could almost forget the unpleasantness in the kitchen. Of course, it would have been easier if Rick hadn't been sitting directly in front of me.

I could feel his eyes on me. This was so annoying. Why did my sister have to arrange this reunion?

He was still staring. "What!" I said looking up.

"Just thinking," he replied cryptically.

I ignored the bait. I was not going there again.

Unfortunately, he went on anyway. "Just thinking about how things could have turned out a lot different if we'd had better communication."

"Well, that could be said about a lot of situations. But don't delude yourself for a second into thinking we would somehow still be together if we were better communicators, whatever that means," I said getting worked up. "We were eighteen, and we had no business trying to plan out our lives together. It wasn't going to work. Those situations never work out." My voice had risen to a fevered pitch during my speech.

"Sounds like you're communicatin' just fine now, Sis," said Dan from the end of the table. His cronies chuckled and high-fived him.

"Shut up, Dan," I snapped and gathered up my plate.

"Look out," he said, "Sis is getting fired up! Hold on to your cups everyone, she's liable to knock 'em all down."

Everyone, including Granddaddy, howled at that one. Geez, you knock one wedding cake over and nobody will ever let you live it down.

I dumped my plate in the trash and stormed off to the house. I locked myself in the pink and blue powder room and sat on the fluffy pink toilet seat cover. I stared mindlessly at the plaque on the wall asking patrons "who sprinkle when they tinkle" to "please be neat and wipe the seat." Why was this getting to me so much? Was seeing an old boyfriend that mind blowing? Maybe there were some unresolved issues, but now was not the time in my life to go digging around in the past. I was focused on my music. Song writing was my great passion. Sure performing was fun, and it paid the bills, but there was nothing quite like writing a song. The process was enthralling to me. Once I started I couldn't stop. I hoped to one day sell some of my songs. That was how I envisioned my musical career progressing—not as some American Idol winning mega-star—but as a songwriter.

There was a knock at the door. "Aunt Diana, I got to poop," said Josh.

"Can't you poop in your bathroom?" I asked, standing up.

"Tiffany stuffed one of her dolls in the toilet."

Great. "Just a minute," I said. I washed my hands and straightened my hair in the mirror. "Time to go home, Diana," I said to myself.

CHAPTER SEVEN

———

The picnic tables had been cleared and my brother-in-law was building an obscenely large fire in the fire pit. It was almost seven and the moon hung low in the star-filled sky. It was a shame I was feeling this way on such a perfect night. I loved a good bonfire. It made me feel young and alive; the smell of smoke, the crackle of burning wood, the contrast of the crisp night air at my back and the heat of the fire on my cheeks. Nothing like it. It reminded me of…

"Are you done pouting yet?" asked Rick as he came up beside me.

"I haven't even started," I said without any real energy.

"Let's call a truce." He held up his hands.

I looked over at him. He was a good person, and we had practically grown up together. I had to give him a break. "Sure," I said with a smile.

"Good." He smiled back. "So Diana," he said in a good-to-see-you-again voice, "what have you been doing with yourself over the last decade?"

"Why Rick," I said playing along, "according to my family, I've been living like a rock star. In reality I'm singing a couple of nights a week, writing songs in my spare time, and paying the bills by temping. How about you?"

"Well, nice of you to ask, Diana," he said. "Until six months ago I was a supervisor on an oil rig working four days a week in the Gulf of Mexico. My wife of two years, Jill, didn't seem to mind the arrangement. It made it a lot easier for her to hook up with her boyfriend from the gym."

"Ouch!" I said sympathetically.

"Yeah, that's what her boyfriend said when I came home a day early and he tripped and fell on the way out of my house," Rick said grimly.

"Tripped, huh?" I said.

"Oh, yeah, he was even clumsier than you." He teased me with a grin.

"And your wife?"

"Took him to the hospital and filed for divorce," he said matter-of-factly.

"Any kids?" I asked.

He shook his head no.

"Wow, I'm sorry to hear that happened to you," I said.

He nodded. "Well, you asked."

"How did you end up back here?"

"My dad wanted to retire and asked me to come home and take over his construction business. Seemed like a good idea to be around family again."

"How's it going?"

"Getting better every day," he replied and squeezed my arm. Before I could protest a blaze fifteen feet high erupted in front of us.

"Woohoo!" Dan hooted. "That there is a fire," he announced, strutting around like rooster.

"What is it with men and fire?" I asked Rick.

"It's dangerous. It can burn you or it can warm you— just like a woman," he whispered in my ear sending warmth spreading in all directions.

Intrigued by his response, I turned to him and said, "So men crave danger and are attracted to dangerous or unattainable women, right?"

"Sounds about right," he agreed, adding, "not me, of course."

"No, of course not. But what happens when you attain the unattainable? When dangerous becomes everyday life? How do you adjust? Or does a man simply start looking for the next unattainable woman?"

He thought about my questions for a moment. I watched the firelight play off his chiseled jaw. Finally, he said, "I don't know about other men, but for me it's not just about the chase."

He turned towards me. "It's about this," he said indicating the bonfire. "It's about putting down roots, raising a family, and going through the adventures of life together that replaces the excitement of danger."

I held his gaze, unsure of what to say. A few seconds ticked by, and he looked back towards the fire. "This was supposed to be us," he said sadly.

I put my hand on his shoulder. "I have to go," I said, standing up. He didn't try to stop me. But I could feel Rick's eyes on me as I made my way over to my sister.

"I have to go now," I said to her.

She nodded. "Can you put Tiffany's car seat in my car on your way out? Dan had it in his truck because he had her over at his mom's house today. I don't want to forget it in the morning rush."

"Sure," I replied. My sister was the great delegator. If you're going that way, can you...? If it wouldn't be too much trouble, could you...? I guess that's how she managed her crazy life.

"The doors are unlocked," she called as I walked back towards the bonfire to say goodbye to everyone.

Granddaddy called me a party pooper for leaving so soon. I reminded him that we had already partied enough last night. Dan asked me if I wanted to do a shot for the road. I declined and thanked him for dinner. The kids clung to my legs and begged me to take them home with me. I didn't blame them. No sign of Rick, though. Well, it was probably for the best. No need for any more drama today. We'd made our peace, and all was well. I headed to Dan's truck to grab the car seat.

Ten minutes of cursing my sister later—who designs car seats anyway, and why are they so hard to take in and out of a car? Argh! What a pain. Rick was leaning against my car as I approached carrying the car seat. "What are you doing with that?" he asked.

"Doing a favor for Ashley, what else?" I said as I marched by him towards Ashley's van which, of course, was parked back near the storage building.

I heard him following me. "Here," he said, "let me help you with that." He took the car seat from me, and I opened the door to my sister's van. It looked like her living room, only there was cereal strewn all over the carpet and sippy cups in all the drink holders. "Wow," he said.

"Yep," I agreed. "This is what having kids looks like."

"They ought to use your sister's car to teach abstinence in schools. Why is this so hard to do?" he asked struggling with the car seat.

"Those things are impossible," I said. "Let me try." I leaned in and peered around the side of the car seat. "Push it through the hole in the back. No, the other one," I corrected.

"Women always say that to me," he joked.

I rolled my eyes. "Sex jokes, really? When we're trying to install a car seat?"

"Hey, you're the one talking about holes," he said. "Got it!" He snapped the buckle into place.

I stood up and came face to face with him. We were both breathing hard from wrestling with the car seat. The interior light timed out, and we were left in the bright moonlight. "Do you know how beautiful you are?" he asked softly.

I didn't move or say a word. I knew I was in dangerous territory. Then his hands were on my hips, and he pulled me in closer. I tilted my head to look up at him. His lips touched mine, and I was suddenly seventeen again. Sure of myself and sure of life. Safe in that little nook of time between childhood and adulthood. My senses were flooded with the feeling that summer would never end, that we would always be young and wild. I could almost feel the sun on my back as his lips caressed mine gently. Then my hands were on his chest, and he wrapped his hands in my hair. His lips left mine and found their way down my neck sending shivers of excitement through my body. I'd like to say just like old times, but honestly this was ten times better than our teenage fumblings. My lips touched his again as his hands found the top button on my jeans. My brain signaled that this was getting out of control, but my body gave an all systems go. I fell back onto the floor of the van, scattering toys and sippy cups. He lowered his body to mine, and I felt his frame hard and unyielding against me.

His mouth found mine again, and he ran his tongue lazily over my lips. Like it was a decade ago and we had all the time in the world. My body ached for him. I wanted to be skin to skin with him. He made quick work of the buttons on my Oxford shirt. His hands found their way to my breasts, and I gasped. I clawed at his shirt, desperate for his skin on mine. He pulled it over his head and tossed it outside the van. *Oh, to hell with it!* I thought and sat up on my elbows. I shrugged out of my shirt and bra and flung them out the van door with a defiant flourish.

There was fire in my blood as the hair on his broad, hard chest teased my sensitized nipples. He pulled away to slide my jeans off, and then I pulled him back towards me hungrily. His delicious, earthy taste and masculine smell filled my senses. Yeah, this was so much better than I remembered. In the distance I heard a dog barking excitedly.

"Hurry," I urged, wanting him in me more than anything else in the world at that moment.

He pulled away to shrug out of his jeans. I heard a rustling outside.

"Rick?" I heard my sister's voice.

Oh no, not now!

"What the hell is going on?" she said shining a flash light into Rick's face.

Dan emerged from the darkness on the other side of her. "Told you they were gettin' busy back here! Someone owes me twenty bucks!" he yelled back to the crowd.

Rick shielded me from view as I searched around for my clothes. "On the ground," I said to his back. He leaned down and threw me my pants and my shirt.

"You might need this," my sister said throwing my bra around Rick. "Sally was running around the yard with it in her mouth," she added.

"Ewww!" I exclaimed dropping the slobbery bra. I pulled my shirt and jeans on and edged around Rick. He pulled on his shirt and buttoned his jeans. My sister shined the flashlight on me. "Put that thing away!" I yelled. "Stop acting like a cop busting some teenagers at make-out point."

"Then stop acting like teenagers at make-out point, and get a room!" my sister huffed. "You know my kids ride around in that van, and you're rolling around having sex in it. Disgusting!"

"No," I said right back at her, "your van's disgusting. I can't believe the health department hasn't condemned it yet."

"I can't believe you two!" she said and turned on her heel.

Dan was laughing and shaking his head. "You should have heard your sister squeal when that stupid dog came running by us with your bra her mouth. The kids started playing tug of war with it."

Rick had been completely silent up until now. "Can you give us a few minutes, Dan?" he asked.

"Oh, sure," Dan said. "Just don't—you know—in the van. I don't want Ashley up my ass about it for the rest of the week." Dan walked away still guffawing.

Rick turned to me. "Don't suppose I can talk you into coming back to my place?" he asked hopefully.

I made a face and shook my head. "Nope. This will do it for me. I need to go home." I was so confused and frustrated. Part of me wanted to follow him home and spend the night wrapped in his arms. You know the parts. And the reasonable part of me thanked God that Ashley interrupted us. What was I thinking? Jumping in a van with an old boyfriend. It made no sense.

"I understand," he said reaching out to stroke my cheek. "That was almost the most amazing sex I've ever had."

I leaned into his hand and kissed his palm. "Me too."

"I want to see you again, Diana," he said.

"I don't know what I want anymore, Rick," I replied softly.

*　*　*

I had a good cry on the way home. As I was going over the bridge, I decided that this little interlude with Rick was nothing more than nostalgia. He was no more a suitable partner for me now than he had been twelve years ago. Sure he was sexier and more charming than egotistical, bossy high school Rick. But he was still fundamentally the same person. And Rick Ellis was not the man for me. I knew that at eighteen. And I knew it now.

After getting an excited sniff over from Max (He seemed to appreciate dog drool much more than I did.), I took him for a quick walk and filled up his bowl. I took a long shower to wash all the grime of the day away and sat in the shower and cried a little more for what might have been. Rick's words were running through my mind on an endless loop. "This was supposed to be us," he had said. Maybe he was right. Maybe we should have had the minivan and the kids on the two-acre lot with the above ground swimming pool. But maybe, just maybe, this was exactly where I was supposed to be.

I gathered up my guitar and pulled a pick from inside my pajama pocket. I sat down on the couch and strummed a few notes, thinking back again to what Rick had said. The fire from that moment still burned in my brain, the nostalgia for lost youth. I picked out a melancholy chord and strummed softly, waiting for the next note to find its way from my brain to my fingers. And there it was. And again. A song took shape. I slowed it down, sped it up, and finally settled somewhere in the middle. I set the guitar down and picked up the yellow pad on the coffee table. The words were easy. I was living them.

*   *   *

I didn't sleep well and woke up bleary-eyed and cranky. Coffee helped, but I was still a little groggy as I made my way towards Greene's Staffing. Mark had asked me to come in at 8:00. to help him before the day started to get crazy. Argh! Mark. I wasn't ready to deal with that situation. The Mark Attraction had simply faded into the background with all that had happened with Rick last night. And that was where I wanted it to stay.

I opened the door to Greene's, expecting some peace and quiet before the phone started ringing. Unfortunately, crazy had already ramped up into full gear at the office. I made my way around a dozen or so light industrial temporaries milling around in the small lobby. Mark was on the phone looking pretty agitated for 8:00 a.m.

"No, Mr. Hagen," he said into the receiver. "I wasn't aware we had a special arrangement with your company that included a thirty percent cash discount. Since when?" He paused. "I see. Did you discuss this with Carol?" Another pause. "Well, I am sorry about the confusion. I will send your team back over right away. There won't be any more cash discounts, though. This is part of an ongoing investigation. Yes, thanks. You too." He disconnected and stood up.

"Okay guys, you can head back over," he said to the temporaries.

They looked at him like he was crazy.

"Yo, man. The bus is gone until noon. We stuck here," said one guy near the door.

"Yeah," another guy with dreadlocks and facial tattoos chimed in. "I told you when you rung me up today that I don't have no wheels."

"No one has a car?" Mark asked incredulously.

"How we gonna afford a car makin' eight bucks an hour?" the man asked. "We legit. We ain't no gangbangers. You find some dude workin' for eight bucks an hour driving a car, and he's hustlin'."

"Where's Miss Carol?" another asked. "She wouldn't have dragged us all the way up here fo' nothin'."

"Carol is recovering from a back injury and should be in on Monday," Mark said looking to me for assistance.

If I had more energy, I would have let him twist in the wind a little longer. "Good morning, Gentlemen," I said pleasantly. "Marcus, right?" I asked the guy with the dreads.

"Yes, ma'am," he responded looking me up and down appreciatively.

"Sorry about the confusion this morning. I'm sure Mr. Greene will make sure you get paid for your time here. Right, Mr. Greene?" I asked.

Mark nodded.

"Okay, so you're going out to Crofton, right?"

"That's right," said Marcus. "Ain't no bus until the 109 at noon."

"If we could get you over to the hospital by 9:00, there's a 108 that will get you to Crofton by 9:30." I looked at Mark. "Okay if I call a couple of cabs to take them to the hospital?" I asked.

"Sure thing," he replied with obvious relief.

Half an hour later all the temps were on their way. Mark touched me lightly on the arm. "Thank you for your help. You were wonderful."

I smiled. It was good to be appreciated by your boss. "Thanks! How did they end up here instead of at work?"

"I pulled them from the assignment. The receivable report shows that Mayfield Manufacturing hasn't paid a bill in three months. They owe over fifty-thousand."

"Wow!" I couldn't believe it. "Who's in charge of collections?"

"Our accountant and Carol," Mark said. "He's supposed to let her know which accounts he's having problems with, and then she gets in front of the customer if necessary to collect. I left a message at Mayfield yesterday, but never heard back, so I decided to get their attention by pulling their workers. Which worked. The manager says he's been paying cash at a thirty percent discount the last three months."

"What!" I cried. "To whom?"

"He said it was to someone identifying himself as Mr. Greene. He thought it was a great way to come in under budget and didn't ask a lot of questions."

"What did the accountant say?" I asked.

"Haven't been able to get hold of him," he said grimly.

"You can't think that Carol is involved in this?" I said, getting riled up.

"No, I don't."

I heaved a sigh of relief.

One that was short lived as he continued. "But it looks like she's been set up to take the fall for this."

"No way. Who would do that?" I asked.

"I have a couple of ideas," Mark replied cryptically.

I paused, on the brink of asking him to share them. But the truth was, Carol had said that she, the accountant, and the Mr. Greenes were the only people with access to the money. If Carol *and* the accountant were both innocent, that left just one person left, and his name had to be Greene. That was one family issue I didn't need to be in the middle of.

I went about getting the office back in shape as quickly as possible. I had just under an hour to get to Mr. Pyres' hotel. I found the message I had taken yesterday before Carol fell still attached to the notepad. I ripped it off and took it back to Mark. I reached out to hand it to him.

He looked me over closely, narrowing his eyes. "What's that?" he asked with a nod to me.

Suddenly self-conscious, I patted my hair and rubbed under my lip to make sure I didn't have smudged lipstick. "What?" I asked.

"On your neck," he said. "Right there." He pointed, and I had a sudden terrible suspicion. "Is that a hickey?"

"Don't be ridiculous," I countered. "Of course not. I have a little bug bite that I scratched. I think Max might have fleas." I scratched at what I hoped was the spot.

He raised an eyebrow. Didn't look like he was buying it. "You're scratching the wrong spot," he said dryly.

"I'm itchy all over just thinking about the fleas," I said. "Never surrender" was my motto.

"Uh-huh," he murmured. "So what did you do last night?"

"Oh," I began. "Took Granddaddy to my sister's, worked on some songs, turned in early. Nothing exciting."

The door opened noisily behind me. "I took this message yesterday," I said handing him the note. "But in all the excitement I forgot to give it to you."

He glanced down. "Great. Just great."

I turned around and headed to the front of the office. A well-dressed man stood at the front counter. "Well, aren't you lovely," he said with a charming smile.

"Can I help you?" I asked, not impressed by the come on. I was a good head above him in heels, and he was just too pretty for me to find him attractive.

"You sure can, sweetie. I'm Mr. Greene," he said.

"What?" I stuttered.

He looked at me like I was addle-brained and spoke slowly, saying, "I am Mr. Greene. The owner. You understand you are working at Greene's Staffing, right dear?"

I nodded. What the hell was going on? "But…" I stuttered, "Mark Greene is here already."

Mark walked out of the back office looking ready for a fight. His mouth was set in a grim line. His fists balled at his sides.

"Oh, no, dear," the man said smugly, flicking imaginary lint off of his expensive suit. "I am David Greene, the owner. That man is an impostor."

CHAPTER EIGHT

"Get out of here, David," Mark growled as he stalked up to the front of the office.

"Oh, no, cousin," David Greene said confidently. "It's you who are going to get out of here."

"I'm here at the request of your father," Mark ground out. "Because you have fucked up every project he's ever put you on." Mark stepped closer, invading David's space.

David waved a hand dismissively. "He's had a change of heart. You know how old people are." He glanced over at me and smiled. "And what is your name, lovely lady?" He put his hand out and, of course, I took it. Impossible to resist, remember.

"Diana," I croaked trying to pull my hand back.

He held it firmly. "I am so glad we are going to be working closely together."

Mark stepped forward threateningly. "Enough!" he yelled. "Get out!"

David removed his coat and walked back to a desk. He laid his brief case down. "I don't think so, cuz," he said removing a paper from the side pocket of the case. "Here's the lease with my name on it. You have five minutes to get out before I call the police. Your services are no longer required."

Veins bulged in Mark's temple as he glanced over the document. He stalked back to his desk and gathered up his things. He came out and towered over David. He set his things down on the desk and placed his hands flat on the desk top. Leaning in he said, "This isn't over. My next call is to Ed, and then to the police. There's some pretty interesting accounting going on around here, and I'm sure you have something to do with it."

David glanced languidly up at Mark the way a cat would eye its prey. "Those are pretty strong allegations, cuz. I'll look into it directly. Perhaps our dutiful office manager knows something about all this?"

Mark banged his hands on the desk. David flinched slightly, but said nothing. Mark grabbed his things and headed for the door without a word to me.

"So sorry for all that unpleasantness," said David. "Perhaps you can help show me the ropes?"

"Well, I'm on an assignment that starts at 10:00, so I need to get going. Mr. Greene…I mean, Mark asked me to come in the first two hours each day this week to cover for Carol until she is back."

"Well, dear, I'm not so sure Carol is coming back, so it looks like the job may be up for grabs." He smiled suggestively. "To the most qualified candidate, of course."

Ick. I shrugged into my coat. "Well, I'll be back first thing in the morning to help you."

"That would be fine, dear," he said walking me to the front.

My phone announced a text message from inside my purse. I scrambled out the door and heard the lock click behind me. From the street I could see him turn the Open sign to Closed and draw down the shades.

I paused to catch my breath at the corner and check my phone. It was Mark.

Meet you at your car

He was leaning against the door as I approached.

"Everything go okay?" he asked.

"Better than it did for you," I responded. "What is going on?"

"That guy is my Uncle Ed's stepson, David. He's been in and out of trouble all his life. The last couple of years I've been hearing from Uncle Ed's wife about how *dear* David is doing so well. It looks like he's wormed his way back into their good graces."

Great. Just what poor Carol needed—another Mr. Greene.

"But why is he here with his name on the lease, if your uncle sent you?" I asked.

"That's what doesn't make sense." He frowned. "I'm a real estate developer, and my uncle specifically asked me to come here and see if there was commercial development potential."

I held up a hand. "You mean he owns the building?" I asked.

"The block," Mark said.

I looked at the prime downtown space. Wow.

"Technically the property is owned by Independent Commercial Partners, Inc.," Mark explained. "My uncle is the majority stockholder. Greene's Staffing, a separate entity owned solely by my uncle, leases the space from the parent company. I can't believe he's waited until now, making pennies on the dollar with the staffing agency and a few tenants."

That fired me up. "Oh, so Mr. Hot Shot Developer was on his way down here to shut us down so he could rake in the big bucks? No concern for all of Carol's hard work or for all the people that depend on Greene's for jobs and for employees."

Mark held up his hands. "Calm down. There will certainly be space in any new structure we develop for Greene's Staffing, if it makes business sense."

"So that's why you're here checking out all the numbers. Seeing if it 'makes sense' for us to keep our jobs," I said hotly. "I have to get to work now. I actually have to work for my money."

He moved aside as I reached for the door handle. He waited for me to settle in and fasten my seatbelt before rapping on the window. I rolled the window down.

"What?" I demanded.

"I need to see you after work."

I cut him off. "I don't think so, Mark."

"You can't keep working for David. He's dangerous."

I rolled my eyes. "I think I can handle pretty boy, in there."

Mark shook his head. "If he's been skimming money from the company, he's got a lot on the line. And desperate people do desperate things," he said leaning in the car.

He looked earnest. He smelled amazing. And he was right. David was a creep. "Okay," I conceded. "Come over at 6:00. I'll make us something to eat. Bring wine and a lot of answers."

"How about a lot of wine and a couple of answers," he teased.

"Don't push it," I warned. "I'm doing this for Carol."

He started to pull out of the window, and then leaned back in. "Diana?"

"What now? You're making me late," I complained.

"That's a hickey on your neck, isn't it?"

I rolled the window up without a word and drove off.

*　*　*

I was dying to call Carol, but I didn't want to be late for The Count, and the ten-minute ride was nowhere near enough time to explain everything that had just happened. I reached the hotel with two minutes to spare. I opened the vanity mirror. Great. A hickey. I dug some cover-up out of my purse and dabbed lightly at the mark. Why was I so stupid last night? I completely let nostalgia and six-pack abs seduce me.

I rushed into the hotel and up to Mr. Pyres' room. He opened the door with a flourish. His bat radar must have detected my presence.

"Ah, Diana, so glad you are here," he said ushering me in. His cape was back to black today. "I must admit that I am excited about today." He rubbed his hands together gleefully.

I wasn't as excited, but I faked it. "Great! Let's get to work. I guess we'll be working down in the office, since all of your information will have to be entered into the computer."

He shook his head. "I have a new attitude, my dear. If I am ever going to meet my soul mate, I have to be open to new experiences," he said with a determined nod. "Even if it means being in the same room as a *computer*." He waved his arm with a flourish, indicating the small workstation containing a laptop and printer next to his giant desk.

"Wow!" I said, impressed. "This will certainly make things easier."

His brow lowered. "Now I have to make it clear that this is only for our special project. I still prefer you work on my manuscripts downstairs. I want no more exposure to those things than absolutely necessary."

I shrugged. I hadn't expected anything less from him. "Okay," I began. "First, we need to set up profiles, including pictures, on a couple of the major dating websites."

"Pictures?" he said with concern. "You want to photograph me?"

I nodded.

"No, no, no," he said dismissively. "Out of the question."

Why wasn't I surprised? "We need pictures to encourage responses. No woman in her right mind will respond without seeing a picture of you." Actually, maybe I had that backwards, I thought watching him settle his cape out around him. "Why don't you want your picture taken?" I asked. This ought to be good.

He fiddled with his pen and quill for a few seconds. "Let's just say I don't photograph well and leave it at that."

The old-fashioned clock ticked off 10:15 over his shoulder. Does he really think he's a vampire? I wondered. Like, as in he has no reflection and doesn't show up in a photo? On impulse I fumbled in my purse and found my phone. I picked it up, flipped it around, and snapped a picture of him before he could protest. He made a strange screeching noise and dove under his desk. I looked at my phone. Man! He was fast for an old guy. Nothing but cape!

"Ms. Hudson!" he said sternly from under the desk. "One more stunt like that, and you are fired! Put the camera away!"

Feeling a little foolish, I dropped my phone back into my purse. "Sorry Mr. Pyres. I just thought you were being shy about having your picture taken. I thought if you saw yourself in a photo, then you would get over the whole photo phobia thing."

He rose from under the desk and flipped out his cape. He stuck a finger with a strange, pointy fingernail at me. "No pictures!"

"Okay," I said meekly. Disproving his delusion that he was a vampire was not worth losing this great paying job. "Let's just start with completing the profile on the first site."

He nodded. I filled out all the basic info, stopping to find out his age, 59, and his height and weight, 5' 10", 175 pounds. I determined he was interested in dating women 35-60 in the Annapolis/D.C./Baltimore area. He had no preferences as far as physical characteristics. So far so good.

"Okay, now we need to tell your potential matches about your hobbies, favorite things to do, etc." I said. "Specific is better. Give examples. So what's your favorite book?"

"The History of Medieval Crockery, Cooking, and Husbandry," he replied.

My fingers paused over the keyboard. I typed *I enjoy experiencing authentic international cuisine.* "How about pets?" I asked hopefully.

"I raise silk worms in Yugoslavia," he replied. "But I don't suppose they count as pets."

I stared at the screen. Close enough, I said to myself, and checked off animal lover. "Any special talents?" I asked.

His brow furrowed in thought. Finally, he snapped his fingers. "I play the hurdy-gurdy quite well."

I shook my head. "The what?"

"A hurdy-gurdy. You know it was used extensively in medieval times and is still popular today. It's a bowed string instrument. It looks like a violin, but sounds something like a bagpipe." He seemed surprised that I had never heard of it.

Actually, I think I had heard the name before, but had no idea what the instrument looked or sounded like. I quickly Googled hurdy-gurdy and pulled up a picture. "That?" I asked, pointing to the screen.

He nodded. "I should have my housekeeper ship it to me. Good call, Diana," he said enthusiastically. "Women are always interested in musicians. You play the guitar, right? Maybe I could sit in on your next gig." He chortled over his use of the musician's vernacular.

I wanted to bang my head on the keyboard. "Next," I said, clicking on the What I Do section. The next thirty minutes went smoothly. He had a strange and interesting resume, but it was perfectly respectable and probably his best selling point.

"Now we need to come up with a paragraph to introduce you. This is important because we aren't using your picture. Women are going to have to like what they read, or they will never contact you."

He walked over to me and handed me a quill and ink written paragraph. "I think that should do it."

I looked at the paper. Incredible. I think he was actually going to get some responses with this. "You're rich?" I asked looking up from the paper.

"Filthy," he replied tapping his fingers on the desktop.

"You know," I cautioned, "you are going to get a bunch of gold-digging wackos by saying you're rich and looking for a soul mate."

"That's where you come in, Diana. To separate the wheat from the chaff."

Wonderful, now I was his wingman. This is not going to be pretty.

We finished up with the profiles around 1:30. I begged off another vegan lunch by saying I had errands to run. He was eager to see if anyone had responded to his profiles and wanted to spend some time 'perusing the lovelies' after lunch. I promised to be back by 2:00 p.m..

I called Carol as I walked down to the coffee shop. "You're never going to believe what happened at the office this morning," I began.

"Some prick named David staged a coup and is claiming to be the owner?" she asked.

"How did you know?"

"Pete, the janitor, saw the closed sign and called me on my cell. I gave him permission to go in with his keys. I got to listen to him get told off by this David character who said, 'Carol doesn't work here anymore' and slammed the door in his face."

"I'm so sorry Carol," I said. I filled her in on the rest of the details about "Mr. Greene" giving discounts to customers and pocketing the cash and the lease mysteriously being in his name now. "Mark's coming over tonight," I finished, "so hopefully he'll have some answers back from old Mr. Greene." I crossed my fingers that those answers didn't include a pink slip for everyone involved. "How's your back?"

She groaned a little. "Better. God, what a mess this is. Mr. Greene was really going to sell the place?"

"I'm so sorry, Carol," I said. "But don't worry. We'll figure something out."

"I wish I had your confidence," she replied wearily. My phone beeped with another incoming call.

"I've got another call coming in. Call me later," I said, and flipped over to the other call.

I didn't recognize the number. "Hello?"

Silence. "Hello?" I said again.

"Diana?" a familiar voice responded.

Oh, no! Not what I needed right now. "Hi, Rick," I said with some annoyance.

"Don't sound so thrilled," he said testily.

"Oh, sorry. I should have said, 'Thanks for the hickey, you jerk!'" Just thinking about Mark seeing my neck made me crazy.

"Sorry. I didn't realize I was giving you a hickey when you were jumping my bones in your sister's van."

"News flash! We're not in high school. No one gives hickeys anymore," I yelled.

I was standing outside the coffee shop, and a snooty-looking woman pointed to the sign on the door that read, "No Cell Phones Allowed." "Bite me," I snapped.

She turned abruptly and stomped into the shop. Great—now I had to find another place to get lunch.

"So biting's okay? Just no hickeys—got it."

"I wasn't talking to you. I have to get back to work."

"No," he insisted. "We need to talk about what happened."

"Nothing happened."

"Something almost happened. I want to see you again." His voice was suddenly soft and silky. It made my toes curl.

"I'll call you later." I hung up before he could protest. I had eight minutes to get something to eat and be back at the hotel.

The Count was pacing the floor when I reached his suite. "Ms. Hudson, you are two minutes late."

I had a bag of chips and a fountain soda from the convenience store across the street. I was hungry, harassed, and stressed. "Sorry, Mr. Pyres. My errands took a little longer than I thought."

He waved his hand around. "Let's get back to work."

I rolled my eyes. Work consisted of looking for soul mates for a vampire. How did I get myself into this?

Surprisingly, there were three messages from interested women. Unfortunately, two of them were obviously prostitutes. "What does she mean when she says she's a submissive?" he asked.

"It means we delete her message," I said.

"What about the one who is talking about her cat?"

I looked at him. Seriously?

"Um, she's not talking about her cat," I said pressing the delete button again.

The third woman was promising. She was fifty, a librarian, and liked to cook. "Let's reply to her," I suggested.

"She's not exactly my type," he sniffed. I cut my eyes at him. "But we should be polite and respond. I agree."

I typed a bland reply. Within a few minutes she had answered back. She wanted to talk on the phone. Yikes!

Mr. Pyres looked scared. "Should I call her?" he asked.

"Depends on if you want to get to know her. But what have you got to lose?" I asked. "This is what dating is all about." God help us all.

"You're right!" he said banging his fist on the table. "I have to take a chance if I want to meet the woman of my dreams. Ms. Hudson, please allow me a few moments alone. I think I had better place this call privately."

I wasn't so sure that it was a good idea. But who was I to say? Look at my current love life. I took his manuscripts down to the hotel office and started to work through the last couple of days. Thirty minutes later the desk manager came over and told me that Mr. Pyres would like me to return to his room.

This time Mr. Pyres didn't open the door before I could knock. In fact it took a couple minutes for him to come to the door. The door swung open and, in a flurry of black cape, The Count announced, "I have a date in an hour, Ms. Hudson. You must help me prepare."

CHAPTER NINE

———

Getting Mr. Pyres ready for his date was easier than I thought it would be. He was so excited about the prospect of meeting the lovely Betty that he seemed almost normal. Or maybe I was just getting used to him. I hoped Betty would be as open to his eccentricities. I tried to get him to ditch the cape, but it was a no go.

"It's a cloak, Ms. Hudson," he said haughtily. "I have no intention of catching my death traipsing about without a cloak."

"How about a jacket instead," I suggested. "You know something that looks normal."

"I assure you that I look perfectly normal for where I come from," he huffed.

And that would be from among the living dead?

I tried another tactic. "Don't you want to make a good first impression on Betty?"

"I believe the best first impression I can make is to be myself."

Okay, he had me there. I shrugged. Maybe Betty was into guys in capes. Hey, stranger things had happened, right? I tried to pull a little more info out of Mr. Pyres after his conversation with Betty. All he said was that her name was Betty Getty, she sounded lovely, and that they were both looking forward to participating in the Annapolis Renaissance Fair in a couple of weeks. They were meeting at a cozy little restaurant near Dock Street for drinks. I gave McGlynn's a plug in case they wanted to go someplace afterwards.

I left Mr. Pyres' hotel at 4:00 with an armload of manuscript pages. I was now two full days behind and would need to work this evening to catch up. Thankfully, there were no new messages on his accounts at the three dating sites. I didn't realize that helping him find love would be quite this time-consuming. I was shocked at the success he was having. It had me thinking about my own love life. If a guy in a cape could find someone, maybe I could too. I paused in mid-thought. Strike that. If that were the case, I'd be on my way to meet a guy in a cape. No thanks. Not worth the risk. I had enough man problems. I didn't need any new complications.

I piled the manuscripts into my car and rolled the windows down. I loved the spring. Anything was possible. Everything felt fresh and new. I flushed thinking about last night. Man, that whole scene had come out of nowhere. What are the chances of running into your high school sweetheart recently off a bad relationship? Not to mention, looking like the world's hottest lumberjack, all hard, chiseled, and grizzled. I had a hickey on my neck and whisker burns on my unmentionables. Damn that dog! It would have been better to just do it and get it out of my system. Put it behind me and move on with my life.

Don't get me wrong. I haven't spent the last decade asking myself *what if.* Just an occasional fleeting thought when I heard an old song or went somewhere we used to hang out. Sometimes I'd hear about him through friends. It always sounded like he was doing great, and I was happy for him. Now I didn't know what to think. I knew I had to deal with this. I didn't see a future for us, but it would be interesting to at least finish what we started last night. I fanned myself. Slow down, Diana. You have another hot man on his way over to see you tonight. I felt like Mae West or something. But then this was how my love life went. No man for months and then two or three cued up and ready to go. Unfortunately, they always seemed to find someone else or turn out to be jerks. And then there was the one that turned out to be married. Argh! But that's another story.

I found a parking space right in front of my condo. Time to get serious and forget about Rick. Mark was on his way over. My priority was paying the bills, so I needed to help him or find a new job. I liked my job temping, and I loved working with Carol, so I wasn't giving up without a fight. And Mark smelled so damn good! Stay on task now. Dinner. I wasn't the world's best cook, but I could make a few decent dishes. I had some frozen shrimp and fresh pasta and cheese. I also had some killer fresh veggies I had picked up over the weekend at Whole Foods.

By 5:00 I had the shrimp thawing, the table set, and Max walked and fed. I had changed into my soccer mom attire—a sapphire blue velour warm-up suit from Victoria's Secret. Hey, it was comfy and sent the right message. This was not a date. Period. I pulled out my laptop and Mr. Pyres' manuscripts. Time to get caught up on the medieval meanderings. Amazing he had a publisher for this stuff. Probably a bunch of guys who wore capes.

I was only one page into the chapter on medieval hygiene practices when my phone rang. My sister. Great, what now?

"I'm working," I said right off.

"I don't care," she said. "Do you know Rick was at my house drunk and mooning over you until 2:00 a.m.?"

Huh, that was worse than I had thought. Secretly, I was a little pleased. "No," I replied. "And it's not my fault."

"Yes, it is," she insisted. "You led him on."

"No, I didn't." Well, maybe a little.

Always the drama queen, she said, "You did, and now he's heart-broken."

"Look, I have a lot going on over here right now. I don't have time to deal with this. My job is in jeopardy, I have a gig Friday that I'm not ready for, and my new boss—who, by the way, may or may not be my legitimate boss—is on his way over."

"You mean the guy Granddaddy called your hottie new boyfriend?" she asked.

"Granddaddy is crazy," I dodged.

"Yeah, but not deaf. He heard you two making out in your apartment."

"We weren't making out, and, besides, it's none of your business!" I yelled into the phone.

"It is when I have your other boyfriend at my house crying in his beer all night."

I rolled my eyes. "Hey, Miss Matchmaker, that was your fault!"

"Grow up, Diana," she shot back. "Stop trying to be a rock star, and get a real life. Find a man. Settle down. Make something of your life before it's too late."

"Oh my God, Ashley, you sound just like Mom."

Ashley gasped. There was no greater insult.

"I do not!" she shrieked. But she did, and she knew it.

"Yep," I said smugly, "I may not have a real life, but at least I haven't turned into Mom. Any day now you'll be feathering your frosted hair and wearing acid-washed jeans."

"You are the worst sister ever!" she screamed and hung up the phone.

Well, that didn't go so well. These spats were pretty normal. But it had been awhile since we had had one this heated. My family, especially my mother and my sister, were constantly waiting for me to get a real life. Like I was some perpetual college student or something. I worked, owned a home, and had a dog. What more did they want? I reached out to scratch Max's head. He glanced up at me with bored eyes and then flipped over onto his back. *Scratch my belly, and make yourself useful, human*, he growled. I obliged for a few minutes which earned me a tail wag and a lick.

I jumped into dinner preparation and by six had everything ready to serve. I was impressed with myself. No mishaps. No mistakes. My doorbell rang, sending Max into a barking frenzy.

Mark stood at the door holding a bag containing two bottles of wine and a bouquet of flowers. Yes, flowers. He was the first man to bring me flowers since, well, since Rick. So much for strictly business.

I invited him in and took the bag with the wine. I wasn't ready to acknowledge the flowers. "Two bottles?" I said. "There better be a lot of answers to go along with two bottles of wine."

He took off his coat and laid it over the back of the couch. "I'm not sure how many answers I have, but I figured the extra bottle might help us forget about the questions for a time."

He stepped closer, and his amazing scent danced into my nostrils. He handed me the flowers. "I know I haven't made a great impression on you. But I promise I will do everything in my power to keep Greene's open. I never came here with the intention of shutting it down."

He was impossible to resist. "I believe you," I said looking up at him.

"I need to ask you a question, and I want an honest answer," he said. I waited for it, knowing what was coming. "Are you involved with someone right now?"

"No," I said emphatically.

"So that's not a hickey?"

I looked away. Well, this was awkward. "Technically I suppose you would call it a hickey," I began. "But I'm not seeing anyone."

"Technically, is that a hickey or not?"

"It is," I said quietly.

He looked like he might snatch the flowers back. "That's what I thought."

"Do you want your flowers back?" I asked looking up at him.

"No, but I'll take a glass of wine now."

"Okey, dokey," I said heading for the kitchen.

Two glasses of wine later and halfway through dinner we were both starting to relax again. He seemed to have let the hickey go, although I caught him staring at my neck a couple of times. So far he had learned almost nothing about why David was now on the lease of Greene's. He still couldn't find any way to get in touch with his uncle.

"I'm waiting for a call back from a friend in Virginia. He was going over to Uncle Ed's house."

Mark also explained how Uncle Ed was thirty years older than David's mother, Marcie. They had married when David was a teenager. Mark's family had been scandalized at first by the age difference and had assumed that Marcie was a gold-digger. But the couple has now been together for over a decade. Their only point of contention was David. He'd been constantly getting thrown out of school and in trouble with the law. Over the last couple of years, though, he seemed to be doing better, and Ed had started including him in more business operations. Things were a little rocky at times, but David had at least been working regularly. It sounded like he had a pretty big chip on his shoulder about Ed even though the man had raised him as a son. As far as Mark knew, David's real father had never been in the picture.

I shook my head. "But why would your uncle put David on the lease and send you here?"

Mark nodded. "I'm not surprised that Ed put him in charge of Greene's, but he would have told me for sure. Which leads me to believe Ed doesn't know anything about it."

"Maybe David's mom did it," I suggested. "Is she a partner?"

"A good possibility," Mark agreed. "She's always trying to help David. There's not much she wouldn't do where David is concerned. And that's what worries me," he added.

"So she goes behind Ed's back and signs the lease over to David. She must have known you were coming here to look at the place."

"Yeah, and I think that's why she did it. She has always been jealous on David's behalf about me. She thinks Ed has given me more opportunities than he has David. Which isn't true. David is ten years younger and has little business experience. No way he's ready for a project like this."

"So, she thinks she's doing David a favor by signing the place over to him, and he thinks he can cover up the fact that he's been stealing from the company by driving you out." I paused. "But David must have realized someone would find out eventually that he was taking the cash, right? It just doesn't make sense."

"By the way," Mark said leaning back and patting his stomach. "This is delicious. You're a great cook."

I glowed. It wasn't often I received praise for my domestic abilities. "Thanks," I replied. "I have a few culinary tricks."

Max gave a little yip from under the table.

"Don't feed him from the table," I warned. "It makes him mean."

Mark cast a wary eye at Max. "More than he already is?"

I reached down to pat Max. "He's not mean," I said with a laugh.

Max growled. I was infringing on his ability to beg food from Mark.

Mark shook his head. "Your dog is weird."

Max growled again and stalked away from the table.

Both our phones rang at the same time. I think Mark's ringtone was a Patsy Cline song. He grabbed it quickly and walked towards the living room.

I answered mine with one hand and picked up dishes with the other. "Diana, I'm coming by tonight." It was Rick. "I'm on the bridge right now."

Oh, geez! "Turn around, Rick. Right now."

"No, we've got to talk about this. I let you get away once, and I'm not making the same mistake again," he insisted.

"This is not happening tonight," I said.

"Then tomorrow," he said. "I'll turn around if you will go out with me tomorrow. A real first date. Dinner. Conversation. No making out in a minivan and no hickeys, except upon request. I promise."

I laughed despite myself. Maybe this was a sign from the universe. "Okay," I said and immediately regretted it. *Forward not backwards, Diana*, I chastised myself.

"Really?" he seemed surprised.

"Yes. Didn't think I'd say yes?" I asked.

"I thought I would have to do a lot more begging and pleading."

"You're not actually driving over the bridge right now, are you?"

"No," he said. There was an awkward pause. "We're still on for tomorrow night, right?"

"Yes, but after 7:00," I added. "I have a lot of work to do."

I hung up the phone. I couldn't believe I had just agreed to a date with Rick. I turned around to wipe off the table. Mark was staring at me. Looked like his conversation had ended a few minutes before mine.

"Did you actually just make a date for tomorrow night with me standing right here?" he asked incredulously.

Well, when you put it that way it sounded pretty bad. "Uh, I guess I did," I stammered.

"With the hickey guy?" he asked.

That sounded worse. I nodded.

"Unbelievable," he muttered.

"Do you want your flowers back?" I asked.

He said nothing and poured another glass of wine. A big glass. I held out my glass for a refill.

He got down to business. "I need you to go in and help David and see what you can find out. Tomorrow's payroll, right?"

I nodded.

"Are you able to process it on your own?"

"I've helped Carol before. I think I can handle it."

"Go in and do payroll and keep your ears open," he said. "But don't antagonize David. I will be in the building in one of the empty spaces. Call me if anything goes wrong."

"Okay," I said. "But what am I looking for? What questions should I ask?"

"Don't ask questions. Just keep your ears open and do payroll. I'll meet you at your car when you leave for your assignment."

"Sounds easy enough," I said.

"I'm pretty sure he's unstable. My friend in Virginia said the house is closed up tight. Looks like even the housekeeper is gone. Ed's secretary said she last heard from him three days ago. He was on his way to meet Marcie for dinner. I told her to send messages to both Ed and Marcie saying that if she didn't hear from one of them by tomorrow morning she was calling the police."

"That should rattle someone's cage," I said.

He nodded. His phone rang again.

"Is that a Patsy Cline ring tone?" I asked.

"No comment," he said and answered the call. "Where are you?" He paused. "And Ed?" Another pause, this one shorter. "Not good enough, Marcie. I've got David here waving a lease at me with his name on it after Ed specifically sent me here to inspect the property." He listened for a response, then shook his head. "No, that was not the deal. Ed has no idea David is here, does he?" I could hear the frustration in Mark's voice. I could hear a woman's voice pleading in the background. "I have to talk to Ed about this. What retreat? Where? Marcie," he said trying to reason with her, "I think David is up to his old games again. There has been money missing the last three months at the staffing company. A lot of money. I'm going to have to involve the police." Mark held the phone away from his ear as she shrieked. "Then get Ed on the phone tonight, or I'm going to the police. I'll be waiting." He hung up the phone.

"Didn't go so well?" I asked.

"Supposedly Ed's at a special retreat to help him relax. A gift from her."

"So she's at home?" I asked.

He nodded. "That's what she said."

"So why would the house be locked up and the housekeeper off?" I asked.

Mark shrugged.

"Mark," I said. "I think Marcie has a boyfriend."

Mark glanced at me. "Well, you are the expert," he drawled.

Ouch. Low blow.

"But that is certainly a possibility," he continued. "But what's signing the lease over to David have to do with any of it?"

"And why would David need to embezzle money from Greene's?" I asked.

"He doesn't need the money, that I know. He has a large salary from Ed's company, a condo, a Jaguar. He's never been a gambler," Mark mused.

My phone rang, and I excused myself and walked back towards the kitchen. It was Carol.

"Hi," she said, "I talked to Mr. Hagen from Mayfield Manufacturing. I called him at home and ended up speaking to his wife who used to temp for us. She pulled some more info out of him. The Mr. Greene he was paying in cash was definitely not David. He said the man was in his fifties and had a southern accent."

I wrinkled my brow. "That's weird."

"Yeah," she agreed. "So how are things going there?"

"A little rocky."

"Wow—you know how to mess up a sure thing, don't you?" she said with a laugh.

"Thanks for pointing that out. It would never have worked anyway," I said defensively.

"You mean your rules about meeting a guy in bar, working with him, etc.?" she asked.

"Yes."

"You know a week ago I was just like you." She paused and added, "No, I was much worse than you. You at least are a Queenie Baby Rock Star." She sounded sleepy, and her words were starting to slur. "I, however, always followed the rules and did the right thing until a couple of days ago. Now, evidently, I get drunk and sing karaoke in public, barf on strangers, and fake injuries. Add in that I did all this in front of my boss who is investigating me for embezzlement, and I say to you: fuck the rules!"

I held the phone away from my ear. "You aren't faking the back injury." I pointed out.

"No, but I faked fainting, which led to the back injury. Karma is a bitch," she said.

"Um, Carol, how many pills have you taken?"

"Clearly not enough. I'm supposed to take two every four hours. I took two at 5:00 and then two more at 9:00."

I looked at my kitchen clock. "It's seven right now, Carol."

"Whoopsie," she said. "Maybe I'll just lie down and take a nap."

"Good idea. I'll talk to you later."

"Scheduling another date?" Mark asked from behind me.

I made a face. "No, talking to Carol who is slightly over-medicated."

"Wish I was too," he grumbled.

I brought him up to speed on Mayfield Manufacturing. "Another wrinkle," he said shaking his head.

We sat down on the couch and stared at each other a moment. I could smell his heavenly cologne from my side of the couch. I had this urge to climb on his lap and sniff his neck. The awkward silence ended with a piercing scream.

Max started barking furiously and jumping at the door.

Someone was banging on my door and shouting, "Help me!"

I raced to the door. A shaken Mrs. Kester stood in the hall.

"Help me!" she pleaded. "There's a vampire at my window. He's trying to get in and suck my blood!"

The entranceway door knob rattled, and I caught sight of a flapping red cape. "Oh, Lord Jesus, save us," she screamed and collapsed to the floor.

Mark had followed me to the door. He stepped out in the hall and glanced at the front door. "Um, there's actually a vampire at the door trying to get in. I think he's calling your name."

I stuck my head out the door. Mr. Vann Pyres had his nose pressed against the glass foyer door and was waving frantically at me.

"Looks like your date got his days mixed up," Mark said dryly.

CHAPTER TEN

———

Police sirens wailed in the distance as I opened the foyer door and stepped outside. "I'm so sorry to disturb you at home, Ms. Hudson," began Mr. Pyres. He glanced around me at Mark trying to wake Mrs. Kester up. "Oh, dear," he said with alarm. "That poor woman looks ill. What happened?"

"She's fine," I said. "Why are you here? How are you here?"

"I do apologize. I called Carol for your address," he said.

And she just gave it to you. Great. So much for employer confidentiality.

"She seemed a bit out of sorts," he said. "Anyway I had to come and tell you that my date is going wonderfully! Betty is the most amazing woman. We are spending tomorrow together, so I'm giving you the day off, but I simply must have my manuscript pages back. Betty is quite the medieval history buff and wants to have a peek at my work." The sound of sirens was getting louder. "Oh, dear," he said. "I hope there's not an accident."

"I'll be right back with your manuscript, Mr. Pyres." I raced up the stairs and hopped over Mrs. Kester, who was just starting to come around. She looked up just as The Count leaned inside the doorway and called, "Do hurry, Diana, we are on our way to dinner, and I am simply famished."

Mrs. Kester shrieked and collapsed again.

"Oh, brother," Mark said as I hopped back over Mrs. Kester's prone form with the manuscript. "This place is a loony bin."

I handed Mr. Pyres his manuscript.

"Thank you so much, Diana. For everything!" He shook my hand warmly. "I will see you Friday," he said and disappeared into the darkness in a flourish of satin red cape.

The police pulled up as soon as I closed the door. Mark had Mrs. Kester sitting up, but she was far from lucid. I opened the door to Officer John. "Wow, Diana, didn't think to see you again so soon," he said cheerfully.

"Yeah," I said, more than a little uncomfortable.

"We had a call from your neighbor again about somebody peeking in her window." He leaned in and said, "I don't know why these old girls think every Tom, Dick, and Harry is peeking in their windows." He laughed. "Now if it was *your* window, then I might believe it."

"Officers," Mrs. Kester croaked, "there was a vampire trying to get in."

John looked at me and then at Mark. "Did she say a vampire?" he asked.

I nodded.

He turned and looked at his partner. "Call a 10-54. Tell them we've got a psych eval."

"Do you really think that's necessary?" I asked. Poor Mrs. Kester. "Maybe she saw something."

"Did you see anything?" John asked.

I looked at Mark. He gave me a look that said I was on my own.

Mrs. Kester settled it for me. "She's brought the devil on this building with all her evil harlot ways!" she shrieked. "I tell you there was a vampire with blood dripping from his fangs trying to break in and get me!"

Maybe a little visit to the psych ward would do her some good. "Nothing out of the ordinary," I replied to John.

"Yeah," John said. "We see this a lot in heavy drinkers. She's probably short on cash this month and going through alcohol withdrawal." He waved a hand. "They'll sort it out at the hospital. Take good care of her, the poor thing." He turned to Mrs. Kester. "You're going to be fine, ma'am," he said loudly.

"I'm not drunk," Mrs. Kester protested. "And there was a vampire." The ambulance pulled up, and in a few minutes they whisked a screeching Mrs. Kester away for evaluation.

"Looking forward to Friday night," said John as he was heading out the door.

"Me too," I said, all too conscious of Mark standing at the top of the stairs.

"Boy, your dance card is filling up quick," he said sarcastically.

"He's a fan," I said brushing past Mark into the apartment. "And he's coming out to see me play on Friday."

Mark made a face. "Seemed like he thinks it's more than that."

"Well, there's not," I said going back for more wine. What another crazy night!

I waved the bottle at Mark. He shook his head. "Unless you're offering me a bed to sleep in?"

"I don't think so."

"Yeah, probably not room in your bed for one more."

I threw a pillow off the couch at him. "Hey!" he exclaimed and threw it back at me. Max started barking and leaping around. Pillows got him excited. And not in a good way. He went right for Mark's leg and had a good hump going before Mark was able to shake lose.

"Even your dog is crazy!" he said grouchily and sat down on the couch. I sat down next to him and tucked my legs up under me.

"I take it the dapper old guy in the cape was your current temp assignment."

"Yep. I told you I was working for a vampire." I smiled.

He laughed. "I know I shouldn't find this funny, but, damn, that was funny! Your poor neighbor." He shook his head. "You owe her a fruit basket or something."

"I do feel bad now. But she's just so mean. And really, maybe she does need a psych eval. Mr. Pyres didn't have blood dripping from his mouth," I added.

"Yeah, but he was wearing a cape and peeking in her windows."

"I'm going to call that semantics," I argued.

"Call it what you will, but that lady will be out to get you when she gets released."

He was right. It wasn't going to be pleasant around here.

Mark leaned down and picked up my guitar from its stand next to the couch. "Play me some Patsy?" he asked, handing me the guitar.

I made a face. "No way."

He thought for a moment. "Okay," he said, "then play me an original."

That I couldn't refuse. It's always more exciting to play your own stuff. I strummed the guitar a few times and checked the tuner. "Here's a fun one I wrote that almost made me famous," I said mysteriously and launched into *The Rum Song*. It was fast and funky with an island feel. It was a great summer song and never failed to get people out of their chairs and on the dance floor.

When I finished, Mark clapped enthusiastically. "Great song! It should be on the radio."

"Everybody says that." I shrugged. "There are lots of songs that should be on the radio but aren't. Most of us just write music and play small venues hoping that one of our originals will get some radio play at some point in our lifetimes."

"Doesn't sound too promising for a career," Mark said.

"I do okay," I replied a little defensively. "Especially in this area during the summer. That song and a few others were featured in a TV series pilot."

"Impressive."

"Yeah, but the show never got picked up. I haven't heard anything from the producers since the fall."

"That stinks," he said. "How did you end up in a series pilot—right place at the right time?"

"Right bar at the right time," I said. "I was playing one Saturday night when a group came in. They heard my originals and, as luck would have it, they were producers looking for a bar to feature in their TV pilot. The next thing I knew I was in a sound booth in California having my songs produced. It was an exciting time. Quite an amazing experience. I met a lot of great people."

"I'm sure a few more boyfriends," Mark teased.

Well, actually he was correct, but I didn't feel the need to share that story. "You're a real comedian. So how 'bout you?

All I know is that you're a commercial real estate developer who may, or may not, be an impostor."

"I don't think my life is anywhere near as exciting as yours," he deflected.

"Oh, no, buddy," I said setting my guitar down. "I think I deserve more details, considering everything that's going on."

He sighed. "I'm thirty-five, never married, and I have an MBA from Georgia State. I had a football scholarship, but tore my knee up in the first season and was never competitive after that." He ran a hand through his hair. "What else?" he stalled. "I starting working for my uncle right out of graduate school and then decided that I needed to do something more adventurous. After a few years, I wanted more stability, so I went back to my uncle three years ago. Anything else?"

I rolled my eyes. "Uh, yeah. You left out all the good parts!"

"Like what?"

"The adventures," I exclaimed.

"Adventures are overrated," he said with a wave of his hand.

I gave him an irritated look. "I just sang you a song," I reminded him. "You can, at the least, tell me about your adventures."

"Some of my former team members that didn't make it to the big time went into the military right out of college. They did four years, got out, and started doing personal security for American expats in the Middle East. They asked me to join them, and I spent five years overseas."

That was adventurous. "So you were a bodyguard?" I asked.

"No, they had the training," he said. "They guarded, and I handled everything else. Logistics, accounting, etc. Not quite as glamorous, huh?"

"So why did you come back?" I asked.

"Just got tired of it," he said and looked away.

I was pretty sure there was more to the story, but I decided not to push. His phone rang, and Patsy started to croon. He looked down. "It's my uncle," he said. He answered the phone, and I took my wine glass back to the kitchen.

Max scratched at the door. I glanced at the clock. It was almost time for his walk. I grabbed my jacket, clipped on his leash and headed outside. We walked around for a long time before His Highness found a satisfactory spot.

When we got back inside, Mark was still on the phone. He ran his hand through his hair distractedly and made a couple of notes on one of the pages in my notepad. "Okay, I'll be there," he said and hung up. He leaned back looking shell-shocked.

"What did he say?"

Mark took a deep breath. "He knows about David, and he's sure that Marcie is having an affair. He said she's been secretive lately, making private phone calls and such. She surprised him with the retreat at lunch a couple of days ago. He's been suspicious the last few months, so he agreed to go in order to catch her in the act. He wants me to come down and follow Marcie. He said he couldn't call me, because they took his phone. He's been trying to bribe the help to get a phone, but no luck."

"Good thing you threatened Marcie with the police."

He nodded. "I think Marcie's plan, whatever it is, is starting to unravel. I'm leaving for Virginia as soon as you're done at Greene's tomorrow."

"Is your uncle okay?" I asked.

"Yeah," Mark chuckled. "He said he feels like he's in a harem. Stuck in the lap of luxury with no way out. Marcie is supposed to pick him up Sunday."

"Which gives her the whole week to hook up with her boyfriend?" I frowned. "That still doesn't make sense. What does it have to do with Greene's?"

"I'll find out tomorrow," Mark said. "Speaking of boyfriends—it's time for you to answer some questions,"

"Oh, really?" I said.

"Who's your date with tomorrow night?" he asked.

Well, that was direct. "My high school boyfriend that, until yesterday, I hadn't seen in over ten years." Right back at you.

That seemed to throw him. "Wow. I wasn't expecting that."

"Me neither."

"So does he have a shot?" Mark asked.

I thought for a moment. "I wrote a song last night about it—want to hear a rough version?"

"Sure."

I wasn't sure what made me offer to sing the song. I never sang an original until it was polished. Maybe I was just trying to avoid answering his question. Or maybe I didn't know the answer. I pulled the pad out of my case where I had scribbled the words last night. I fiddled with my guitar a few seconds and started to sing. I glanced up at Mark a few times to gauge his reaction, but his face was a mask. Singing the song for the first time since last night reignited my turmoil over Rick.

I finished the song awkwardly, adding, "I'm still working on it."

Mark said nothing. He reached down to pet Max. I was getting ticked. "If it sucks, just say so," I said setting my guitar down.

"It was great," he finally said. "It made me think about things I haven't thought about in a long time."

"That's what it does for me too," I said feeling mollified.

He leaned closer and said, "Diana, I think you are the most amazing songwriter. Thanks for giving me a private show." He kissed me lightly on the cheek and patted my hand. He stood up and stretched. "I should get going."

What the heck just happened? A peck on the cheek? A pat on the hand? "Okay," I said standing up. "Is something wrong?"

"Nope," he said. "Your song just made me realize that your date tomorrow is more than just a date."

I wrinkled my brow. "What's that supposed to mean?"

"It means that I would love to chase you around this apartment the rest of the night," he said, stepping closer. "And I like to think I'd probably catch you. But when that happens I want it to be just the two of us."

That irked me. Did he think I was an old maid pining away for lost love? I put my hands on my hips. "First of all," I began as I followed him to the door. "There was no way you were going to 'catch' me tonight." He raised an eyebrow, but said nothing. "And second, if you had done a good enough job of it, my old boyfriend wouldn't have been on my mind. Really," I added sarcastically, "if the women you sleep with have a problem keeping their minds off old boyfriends, then maybe you should work on your skills a bit."

He started to say something but stopped. He turned and grabbed me by the waist and pulled me against his chest. I was immediately enveloped in the scent I was starting to think of as 'manly spice and everything nice'. They should make a candle scented like a good-smelling man. His lips brushed mine, and my stomach flipped and flopped. I pressed against him and returned the kiss hungrily. Old boyfriend? What boyfriend? He pulled away first.

"My skills are just fine," he said looking down at me.

Yes, they were, I silently agreed.

"I'm not worried about right now," he continued. "I'm worried about later."

I looked up at him. "I wasn't thinking about Rick just then. What makes you think I would later?"

"Your song," he said and kissed my forehead. "I'll see you tomorrow."

CHAPTER ELEVEN

———

After another sleepless night, I pulled myself together and got ready for work. My mood lifted when I took Max for a walk and stepped out into the brilliant sunshine of a promising spring day. After taking care of payroll I had the rest of the day to myself, and I had a date that I was actually looking forward to tonight, despite what Mark had said. I wasn't stuck in the past or trying to recapture my lost youth. Okay, so I wrote a song about recapturing lost youth with an old boyfriend. It didn't mean that was how I felt *now*. Like many songs I wrote, it was how I felt at a moment in time. I liked to capture those feelings with a song. It's how I wrote.

The only black spot on my otherwise promising day was the precarious position of my employment. "What ifs" swirled in my head as I made my way to Greene's. What if David Greene really was the new boss? What if Marcie had some master plan to steal from the company? What if old Mr. Greene did decide to sell? I could envision a dozen scenarios, but none of them spelled job security for me right now.

I stopped in at Shack's and grabbed a cup of coffee. I decided to have whipped cream on my latte. It was one of those kinds of days. I reached Greene's at 8:00 a.m. The doors were still locked, and the blinds were closed. I used my key and went in.

Carol would freak if she saw the place; it was a mess. Timesheets littered the floor around the fax machine. Files had been pulled out of the cabinets and stacked haphazardly on the desks. The coffee pot was still on, and the blackened residue permeated the air. I sighed. This was going to take a while. I set about cleaning up and organizing as best I could. The coffee pot was beyond repair. The phone rang, interrupting the quiet.

"Do you know there were twenty-five messages on the machine this morning?" Carol asked.

"Well, good morning to you too," I said. "Sounds like you have finally risen from the dead."

"Yes. Other than a slight headache, I am up and moving. I checked the messages from home this morning and couldn't believe it! What's going on there?"

I brought her up to speed on Mark's call last night from Mr. Greene and the current state of the office.

"I'm coming in," she said with determination. "If that idiot wants to fire me, he can go ahead."

"Not a good idea," I warned. "Manage what you can from home, but wait until Monday before you come in. Give Mark a chance to get to the bottom of everything this weekend."

"Speaking of Mark," she asked, "how did things go last night?"

"Um, not real well," I conceded. "He thinks I'm hung up on my old boyfriend, Rick."

"The one from high school?"

"Yeah."

"That's weird. Why would he think that?"

I paused. "Because I'm having dinner with Rick tonight."

"What? Since when?" Carol asked.

I sighed. "It's a long story. I'll catch you up later. I need to get payroll started."

"Geez. I'm out a few days, and everything goes wacky."

Fifteen minutes later I had cleaned up as best I could and was attempting to organize the timesheets for payroll. The front door opened, and in strode David dressed in an expensive suit and acting like he owned the place. Which, I guess at this moment, he did.

"Ah, the lovely Diana," he said breezing past me on his way to the back office. "Thank you so much for coming in and taking care of things."

I nodded, doing my best to look like I had no idea that he was swindling the company, and went back to working on payroll.

A few seconds later he popped his head out. "Is there any coffee?" he asked.

"The coffee maker is out of commission," I said.

"Oh," he replied. "Be a dear and run out and fetch me a cup at the coffee shop."

I stared at him. In all my years temping no one had ever asked me to fetch them a cup of coffee. Fetch like a dog. Just keep it together until Mark can get rid of this guy, I told myself. "How do you take it?" I asked between gritted teeth.

"Black's fine," he said as his cell phone buzzed.

I grabbed my purse and headed for the door. A text came through on my phone. It was Mark.

Mark: *How's it going?*

Me: *He's making me go get him coffee :(He's an ass!*

Mark: *Grab me a cup, too.*

Me: *You're an ass, too!*

As I reached the front of the office the door swung open, and in walked Thomasina/Thomas Deville in all her/his glory. I hadn't seen Thomasina in about six months. We were pretty sure that Thomasina was technically a man. However, he had habit of randomly showing up dressed as a hooker and calling himself Thomasina. This didn't go over well with customers. When he was in Thomas mode he seemed like a normal, although slightly effeminate guy. He was fairly dependable, all things considered, but Thomasina had a habit of showing up at the worst possible moments. Like when the president of Mayfield's parent company decided to tour the facility, and Thomasina came to work instead of Thomas, dressed in lime green hot pants and a blonde wig. Carol had been burned a couple times by the cross-dressing temp. Although she had never technically fired him, she only sent him out on assignments if she was desperate. Thomasina also lacked the basic professionalism that Thomas possessed.

"Hey, girrrrl," she drawled. "Where Miss Carol at?" She sashayed up to the front counter and plopped her big sack purse down.

"She's out sick," I said trying to move her back towards the door.

"Oh, that's too bad," she said and then paused dramatically and raised her hands in the air. "I got to ask Jeezus to heal Miss Carol! Take the devil from Miss Carol, Lord! Amen! Sista!" Her eyes closed when she felt The Lord moving her. She opened one fake eyelash ringed eye at me. "Can I get an 'amen,' Sista?" she asked with attitude.

Oh, brother. "Amen," I said.

"Praise Jeezus," she murmured.

"Can I help you with something?" I asked, still trying to move her towards the door.

She rolled her eyes and pursed her mouth. "I got a problem with you people," she began. "My brother, Thomas, says you won't give him a job. He says it's because of me."

I just stared at her. Let them talk it out of their system, Carol always said.

"Now I told my brother that Carol has always liked Thomasina. She just hasn't had any positions that match my *particular* qualifications. I guess we should have checked with Carol before I filled in for Thomas at the factory."

I nodded. This was a new development. Thomas was trying to get back in Carol's good graces by pretending Thomasina was his sister. "So you're saying that you're not Thomas?" I asked and then cringed at my rookie mistake. Never challenge their delusions, just pretend that everything they say is completely logical.

"You sayin' I look like a man!" she shrieked at me. One eyelash fell off and floated to the floor like a butterfly. Her wig was slightly askew. Things were starting to get out of hand.

David called from the back, "You back with my coffee, Diana?"

I smiled. "I'm pretty new here, so maybe you should talk to the owner. He can help you while Carol's out." I pointed to the back office.

Thomasina gathered up her purse and slung it over her shoulder. "Oh, I got somethin' to say to the owner," she huffed as she tottered to the back on three-inch stiletto heels.

I heard David calling my name a few seconds later as I walked out the front door to go get coffee. I was pretty sure there would be a long line at Shack's.

My phone rang as I crossed the street to Shack's.

"I love those boots," said Mark.

I flushed and looked around. "You're spying on me?"

"I'm upstairs," he said. "And I'm not spying. I'm admiring."

"Oh, I'm sorry," I said sarcastically. "I'm so hung up on my old boyfriend I hadn't noticed."

He laughed.

"What do you want?" I asked.

"I wasn't kidding about the coffee. Cream no sugar. Just leave it on the landing," he said.

"You're a jerk," I said and hung up.

* * *

After finishing a cup of coffee and perusing the local paper, which contained a mention of my upcoming performance at McGlynn's in the Entertainment section, I headed back to Greene's with two lukewarm cups of coffee in hand. I left Mark's next to the stairs and headed into the office. A trail of blond wig hair littered the floor along with a lime green stiletto and what looked like a gold lame tube top. David barreled out of the back office. His eye was starting to swell, and his suit was stained with what looked like makeup.

"You!" he yelled at me. "You sent that that…," he sputtered for the right word, "person back to me! I should fire you right now."

"She wanted to speak to the owner," I said innocently.

"She attacked me! Look at my face!" he said.

"Huh," I replied, "she's never been violent before. What did you say?"

"I said what any sane person would say: We don't hire transvestite prostitutes. Now get out of my office!" He dabbed at his eye with a paper towel.

I made a tsking sound. "Probably shouldn't have said that. What'd she do? Hit you with her purse?"

"After she leapt over the desk and attacked me. No wonder this place isn't worth a dime. The sooner I get rid of it the better," he muttered. "I'm going back to my hotel to change and have lunch. Lock up when you're finished." He grabbed his coffee on the way out.

So much for keeping my eyes and ears open. All I'd learned that morning was that David liked black coffee and didn't like dealing with temps.

On the other hand, that left me alone in the office…

I glanced out the front window. I had no idea if David would come back, but I figured it would take him at least an hour to get to his hotel and change. I slipped into the back office, surveying the mess of paperwork David had left sprawled all over the desk. Receipts, time cards, payroll stubs, work orders. Carol might faint for real if she saw this. I quickly did my best to sort through the mess, looking for anything incriminating.

Unfortunately, I had no idea what that incriminating thing might be. I found a receipt for two reams of printer paper—probably not a smoking gun. Under a stack of time cards there was a work order for Mayfield Manufacturing, not, I noticed, noting any sort of cash discount. I arranged a dozen or so reports that looked a lot like the ones I'd seen Carol stressing out over, but I honestly didn't know how to read them well enough to know if these books were cooked or not. I was just about to give up, when I spied something shiny sticking out from under a pile of pink phone messages. I grabbed it, finding a silver USB flash drive. Okay, chances were slim that it contained a typed confession from David about exactly what he was doing, why, and how to stop him. But for lack of a better plan, I popped the drive into the computer, then clicked to open the files on it.

Unfortunately, they hadn't been made on this computer, as a window popped up telling me that the computer had no idea how to open this particular type of file and would I like it to search the internet for the appropriate type? Hey, if the computer wanted to be that helpful, who was I to argue? I hit "okay" and waited, one eye on the doorway. I didn't know how long I'd been in here, but even David couldn't take too long to change. Finally the computer told me that it had found the program— some human resources software—and it told me I needed to download an update to open these files. Oh, geeze. I clicked "okay", suddenly taking The Count's negative view of these "infernal devices" as I waited again. A negative view that only grew when the update froze halfway through.

I took a deep breath, thought some dirty words, then yanked the stick from the computer.

Which, in hindsight, might have been a hasty move. A window immediately popped up on the computer screen telling me that I had made a "critical error" in removing the disk halfway through an update. Oh crap. I quickly plugged the drive back in and tried to click on a file again. It opened…but only displayed lines of nonsense and random characters. Sure enough, whatever data had been on the files before, it was totally corrupted now.

Great! I find one *possible* piece of *possibly* incriminating information, and what do I do? Ruin it before I even know what it is! I could practically hear Ashley's sarcastic voice in my head, telling me, "Way to go, Diana!"

I put the useless flash drive back under the stack of messages, then moved all the papers back into some semblance of the chaos I'd first encountered in the room and quickly slunk back to the main office to finish payroll.

I was able to get it done by 10:30, and there was still no sign of David. But I figured that since Carol would take care of any problems that came over the phones, and she had computer access from home, it was probably just as well to leave the office closed today. It reduced the chances of further brawls with transvestite-prostitutes in the middle of the office.

Mark was waiting outside my condo. "What the hell happened to David?" he asked. "I saw him leave and followed him back to his hotel. He looked rough."

"A transvestite named Thomasina beat him up while I was out getting coffee," I said.

Mark howled. "Man, I wish I could have seen that," he shook his head in wonder. "I love that office."

I looked around. "Any sign of Mrs. Kester?" I asked.

"Nope. They'll probably keep her there a day or two."

Maybe I should have had Thomasina pray for Mrs. Kester instead of Carol. Mark followed me up the stairs and into my condo. Max greeted him with friendly doggie hug which quickly turned into a too-friendly hump.

"Hey, he really likes you," I said.

"Great," he replied, kneeing Max away. "I wanted to talk to you before I go to Virginia."

"Oh," I said with sarcasm. "I think you pretty much said it all last night."

"I forgot one thing," he said taking hold of my hands and stepping in closer. I took advantage of the close proximity and inhaled.

"Yeah?" I said.

"I want a date, too."

I narrowed my eyes. "What?"

"I want to throw my hat in the ring," he said. "I like you. You're beautiful, talented, smart. Very sexy."

"Keep going," I purred.

He laughed. "I've decided I don't want to sit back and wait for your old boyfriend to sweep you off your feet."

"Oh, really," I said. "And how do you know I would even go out with you? After all, I met you in a bar, and I work for you. Two big no-no's in my book."

"You don't technically work for me, and I think after all we've been through so far together you can overlook meeting in a bar," he said.

I thought for a second, and then I leaned in for another sniff. Irresistible. "Okay," I said. "I have an opening on my dance card for Saturday night."

"Wow. I thought I would have to do a lot more persuading." He pulled me in closer.

"I'm open to more persuading," I whispered against his neck. Mark's lips brushed mine.

"You'll have to wait until Saturday," he whispered back.

I swatted him on the arm. "Rat!"

He laughed and jumped out of the way. "I'll call you tomorrow with an update."

"Go!" I said. "Before I change my mind." I started to push the door closed on him.

He leaned back in. "Diana," he said with a grin.

"What?"

"Do me a favor? Try to keep it down to just the one hickey."

"Go!" I said slamming the door.

I spent the rest of the morning piddling around my apartment and noodling on my guitar. I didn't look at the song I'd written the other night. Didn't want to go there right now. I updated my website and Facebook with my latest gig schedule and uploaded a couple of pictures. I wasn't a super social media techie like some performers, but I tried to keep the basic info updated. I made a trek to Whole Foods early in the afternoon and restocked my kitchen, such as it was. I had a text from Rick at 3:00 p.m. asking for my address and saying he was looking forward to tonight. I was looking forward to it too. I wanted to catch up and hang out. Maybe reminisce about old times. But I definitely did not want to end up in the back of a van again. Metaphorically speaking, of course.

At 6:00 I stopped what I was doing to get dressed and primp. Just a little primping, mind you. I wasn't sure where we were going, so I decided to err on the dressier side and went with a cute little black dress and heels. I started to put my hair up, and then I remembered Rick's hands in my hair in the van. And the way he used to wind it around his fingers when we were lying in bed. I ran a flat iron through it instead until it looked like spun gold. He was driving all the way from Dover, I rationalized. I certainly didn't want to disappoint him.

Max eyed my dress and hair with disdain. I swear the dog knew I was going somewhere, and that he was not invited. At 6:45 I heard a car pull up downstairs. I looked out the window. Oh, no. Mrs. Kester was back. There was a younger man with her helping her out of the car. She was angrily waving him off. Rick pulled up right next to them. This ought to be good. Rick reached the foyer door first. He was knocking at my door a few seconds later. I tried to open the door and pull him in. But the second I opened the door, he ran back down the stairs to help Mrs. Kester through the foyer door.

"Just keep your hands to yourself, boy," she said to the man with her.

"Mom, I'm just trying to help. The doctor said you would be a little unsteady on your feet until you got used to the medication," he said patiently. Then he added, "Thanks," to Rick who was holding the door for them both.

Mrs. Kester looked up at Rick and then at me. "Got yourself a different one tonight, I see," she snarled. "Like a revolving door—old ones, young ones. You name it! And don't think I don't know what you did last night."

Awkward. "Hi, Mrs. Kester. How are you feeling?" I asked.

"Don't 'hi' me you little trollop!" she yelled.

"Now Mom, be nice," her son said.

"Shut up," she snapped at him.

I'm sorry, he mouthed, as he opened her condo door. She gave me an evil look and went inside.

Rick raised an eyebrow. "That was weird."

"Yeah, she's not been well," I said making the cuckoo sign next to my head and walking into my condo. "The ambulance had to come pick her up yesterday."

"So she was seeing strange men with you last night?" he asked following me.

"She thought she saw a vampire peeking in her window and called the police."

He made a face. "And what about 'old ones, young ones'?"

I shrugged. "Want some wine?"

He shook his head but let it go. "Sure," he said and bent down to pat Max. "Hey, little puppy."

Max looked at him for a minute and gave his pant leg a sniff. He tolerated the pat on the head, but he was clearly not impressed. He turned around and went to lie down in his bed. That was strange. Max never turned down a fresh leg to hump.

"Cute dog," Rick said. I handed him a glass of wine. "And beautiful lady. To first dates," he said, raising his glass to mine.

"I'll drink to that," I said with a smile.

CHAPTER TWELVE

———

Rick had made reservations at an upscale restaurant on the waterfront. The sun had already set by the time we were seated at our table with a view of the bay, but there was still a pretty glow to the sky. There was a wood fire crackling in the over-sized fireplace in the center of the room.

"This place is amazing," I said looking around. "I've never been here before."

"Good. I tried to pick somewhere that you hadn't played. I asked your sister, but she made it sound like you were at a different bar every night." He shook his head. "She's something. So I ended up checking your website and made sure I picked someplace that wasn't listed."

Impressive effort, I thought. "Thanks. I appreciate that. I don't usually get to try new places. When I'm not working, I'm usually home."

"Not out with a wide age range of men?" he teased.

I made a face and stuck out my tongue.

He shook his finger at me. "Better watch it. My Nana says your face will get stuck like that."

"Your Nana was mean to me. She said I was trying to trap you into marriage."

"Guess she was wrong about that," he replied.

Awkward silence. "So how's the construction business?" I asked.

"Better than working on an oil rig, and if this economy improves a little it might just pay more."

"Yeah, it's been a tough couple of years," I agreed. "I lost a lot of private gigs when the market nose-dived."

We placed our orders and continued to make small talk. He was into the business side of contracting. He had quite a few ideas about how to improve and streamline the operations. I had never seen this side of him before. In high school it had always been about football and getting into the best college. We talked about my music career, and he complimented me on my Facebook fans.

"You've got a lot of people who come out to see you," he said.

"I've been playing around here for five years so I've developed a decent following. It helps pay the bills." I toyed with my glass of wine and looked out the window.

"I'd love to come see you play," he said with genuine interest.

"That would be great," I replied rather noncommittally. I wasn't sure where this was going and didn't want to encourage future contact until I was sure.

He leaned over and took my fidgeting hand. "Relax, enjoy the night. Let's just see what happens," he said. He had piercing dark eyes and it had always seemed that he could look right through me.

I looked away first.

He leaned back. "Second thoughts on this date?"

I shook my head no. "I'm worried about getting stuck in the past. I don't want the same relationship we had in high school. If that's how it's going to be, then I'm not interested."

"Me neither," he said emphatically. "I want the woman that you've become—the talented, sexy, sassy, slightly less clumsy woman. Not the girl I knew in high school."

I relaxed a little and gave him a smile. "I don't know if this is going to work out."

"Let's just give it a try and see what happens," he said putting his hand over mine.

I smiled. "Hey, Rick, when was the last time you lost at pool?" I asked changing the subject.

He squinted his eyes and furrowed his brow. "Must've been twelve years ago to a skinny blond with an amazing bank shot."

"I've still got that bank shot."

"I don't doubt it," he said. "But I spent six years on an oil rig with a bunch of guys with nothing better to do than play pool and watch TV."

"I think I can give you a run for your money." And I meant it. I was good in high school, but having spent years working in bars for a living I had played more games of pool than I cared to count.

"Is that a challenge?" he asked.

I nodded.

"How about strip pool?"

I made a face. "No such thing!"

"Winner takes all—when we get back to your place." He laughed.

I rolled my eyes. "Do you always work so hard to get your dates naked?"

"Well, technically I had you naked night before last, so it shouldn't be so hard a second time," he said smugly.

Thirty minutes later we were on our way down to Dock Street to a little tavern called Brown's. No one remembered why it was called Brown's. The current owner, Debbie, had bought the bar from Mr. Turner, who had no idea where the name came from either. It was a dive bar with a capital D. The faint smell of cigarette smoke still clung to the low ceilings and ripped black vinyl stools despite the decade long smoking ban. It was so dark you could hardly see the floor—not that you would want to. It had a U-shaped bar in the middle and pool tables and a shuffle board in the back. I had played here a couple of times, but it wasn't my crowd, and the pay wasn't great.

It was almost nine and the place was starting to get busy for a Thursday night. All the regulars had staked out their bar stools earlier in the day. "Hey, there stranger," Debbie called from behind the bar. "Long time no see. Oh, looks like you've brought Mr. Tall, Dark, and Hot with you."

I rolled my eyes.

"You're going to give him a big head, Debbie," I said.

"He looks like he has a big everything." She cackled and a few patrons joined.

"Looks like you're pretty lucky to be with me, girlie," Rick teased against my ear. His breath tickled my neck, and I shivered. Debbie was right. Rick was hot, and he had a big everything.

Rick bought two beers at the bar and then we made our way back to the pool tables. They were all in use, so Rick laid a stack of quarters on the rail of the nearest table.

A small guy with beady eyes paused mid-stroke and said, "This table is partners only." He had a big piece of chew in his mouth and a Styrofoam cup was positioned close by.

His partner took in Rick's stature and said, "Hey, Jonesy, this is a friendly game. There's room for all."

Completely cool Rick said, "Hey, no problem. I've got me a beautiful partner right here." He nodded to me.

Jonesy spit in his cup and gave me a hard look. "Ain't playin' no girl pool tonight," he said and made the last shot of his game. His partner high-fived him.

See here's the thing. I've been working in bars for years, so Old Jonesy didn't faze me. Normally I would just laugh it off and move on to the next table, but I hate being called a girl. So against my better judgment, I slipped out of my jacket, revealing more than a little leg in my little black dress. I hung up my coat slowly while all the guys watched and then wandered over to the rack of pool sticks. I tried a few before I found one I liked, and then I walked back up to the table.

"Well, unless you'd like to forfeit to us, it looks like you're out of luck. That's our money," I said pointing to the quarters on the rail. "And you and your friend here are the winners so you play us next. Eight ball, right?"

Jonesy eyed me for a moment and spit in his cup again. His partner was racking up the balls. Jonesy turned to Rick. "Hey big guy," he said in a challenging tone, "you mind keepin' your woman in line."

Rick smiled and shook his head. "It ain't that easy, Jonesy."

Jonesy looked at me again. "Play for money to make it worth my while."

I chalked my stick and said, "You really don't want to do that, Jonesy." I leaned over, took a steady aim, and whacked the cue ball. The ten and fourteen went in. I looked over at Jonesy and said, "Looks like we've got the big balls."

I cleared half the table on my first turn and when Jonesy missed on his second shot, Rick finished it off. Jonesy huffed and puffed and then headed up to the bar to sulk. "Hey, how about we play for money now?" I asked brightly.

"Now you're just showing off." Rick smiled.

"I really don't like being called a 'girl' by a male chauvinist red neck," I replied. I took a swig from my beer. "Wrack 'em up. Now the real fun begins. I'm going to kick your ass!"

We had a blast. He was a gracious loser, even when I beat him three out of four games. We put our sticks away and got two more beers from the bar. "You really have been spending too much time in bars," he said leaning in for a kiss. It was light and noncommittal, kind of like the date.

"Let's go find some music on the jukebox," I said grabbing his hand.

Brown's jukebox hadn't seen anything new in years. That suited us just fine. I picked a Mary J. Blige song. He picked Nickelback, I picked Train, he picked Rage Against the Machine.

I had to say something about that one. "You still like that stuff?" I asked.

"Only moments like this."

"How romantic," I said with sarcasm.

We continued to flip through, and then we both stopped and stared. For a second neither of us said a word. "I gotta do it," he said softly as his hand pushed the button for Alicia Key's hit *Fallin'*.

As the music began, he closed his hand over mine and pulled me over to the small empty dance floor. We rocked gently to the music, the words rolled around us. I leaned against his chest and felt his arms tighten against me. His lips brushed my forehead. "Remember the last time we danced?" he asked softly.

"The beach after graduation," I said.

"I remember the stars in the sky and your hair looking like gold in the moonlight. I felt like that was the beginning of the rest of our lives," he said wistfully.

I remember feeling trapped. Like someone else had decided my life for me while I was asleep, and all there was for me to do was wake up and live it. "It was a beautiful night," I agreed.

He pulled away and looked down into my eyes. "Sounds like we were thinking different things that night."

"Do you want to re-hash all that right now?" I asked with a sigh. "I thought we were moving forward."

"I guess I want to know where I went wrong so it won't happen again."

Classic Rick, I thought. Let's analyze everything to death. Alicia was gone and Rage Against the Machine was blaring across the speakers. How appropriate. We sat down in an empty corner booth. I brushed my hair out of my eyes, wishing I had pulled it back tonight. "So what went wrong," I said fiddling with my beer label. "Where should I start?"

Rick's face darkened. "Oh, come on. It wasn't that bad."

"For you," I shot back. "You had your life all planned out and expected me to tuck my life in around yours wherever it would fit."

"You didn't have a plan," he said with exasperation. "You were going to major in music in hopes of becoming the next Carly Simon. At least economics was a real degree."

"I hated economics," I hissed. "And thanks to you I ended up at a school that didn't have a music program at all. So I spent four years in classes I was bored to death with. Luckily there was a decent music scene on campus."

"Oh, yes," he said with sarcasm. "Your grunge music buddies. I wonder where they all are now?"

"Grunge was in back then," I said defensively. "And from what I see on Facebook, they're doing just fine."

Rick rubbed a hand across his face. "Look," he said quietly, "I don't want to fight. I just wanted to know where it went wrong."

"I'm not sure it was ever right," I said sadly.

The ride back to my house was quiet. Rick commented politely as we passed different landmarks. I was tired after my long crazy week and more than a little disappointed. Rick was so sexy and so interested in me, but just the thought of being in a relationship with him again made me feel claustrophobic.

"I'm worried that you're going to try to change me again," I blurted out a block from my condo.

He glanced over at me. "I think you're perfect, Diana," he said with a smile.

"Yeah, right now. But what about six months from now? What if this gets serious? Are you planning on moving to Annapolis?"

Rick pulled up to the curb in front of my condo. "I don't know what will happen in six months. But if we got to that point, then I'm sure we would work it out," he said reasonably.

"I'm afraid you'll try to take over my life. Tell me to get a real job," I said.

Rick stared straight ahead his hands on the steering wheel. "Well," he said cautiously, like a man wading into alligator-infested waters. "What are your plans? Do you see yourself at fifty still playing in bars? What about children?"

"I can't imagine not playing for an audience," I said. "So, yes, I see myself playing in bars at fifty. And I definitely want kids."

Rick rolled his eyes.

"I saw that Rick Ellis," I said. "It's driving you crazy. You're thinking 'she has a degree, why doesn't she get a real job?'"

He turned to me. "I didn't say that. You're putting words in my mouth."

"I'm going to continue to write songs and play out and look for opportunities to develop this into a full-time career. In case you didn't know, my songs were featured in a TV series last summer. They were professionally produced."

"Oh, I know all about last summer," he said. "Your songs were featured on a pilot that was never picked up, and you had an affair with some B-rated actor."

I shrieked. "I don't know where you get your information, but you are completely wrong! This date is over!" I jumped out of the car and crossed the lawn as fast as my high heels allowed.

He left the car running and followed me cursing all the way. "Jesus, Diana, slow down." He caught me at the door. "I'm sorry!" he said putting his hands on my shoulders and turning me to face him.

"This was a bad idea, Rick," I said.

"No, we're just going through a rough patch. It was a great evening."

I shook my head. "This isn't going to work."

"It has to work," Rick said with passion. "Ever since I saw you again, I can't stop thinking about you." He wrapped his arms around my waist and pulled me close. He felt warm and safe. I let myself snuggle against him for just a moment. "I love you, Diana," he said. "I never stopped loving you."

I pulled away. How could this be happening? "You loved me at eighteen, but you don't even know me now."

"Then let me get to know you now," he entreated. "Give me another chance."

Great, I thought, here I am with yet another drama playing out on my front lawn. Mrs. Kester's light was off, but I was sure she was crouched by her window listening. I was tired and confused. "I had a great time for the most part tonight. Let's just call it a night, and we'll talk later."

He nodded, but looked reluctant to leave.

"Thanks again," I said leaning up and kissing him on the cheek.

"Were you ever in love with me?" he asked.

His question threw me. I certainly had thought I was in love with him at the time. "I'm not sure," I said quietly.

He nodded and walked back to his truck.

CHAPTER THIRTEEN

———

It was a rainy, gray morning, and it suited my mood just fine. I had tossed and turned most of the night thinking about the ugly scene with Rick. I had three text messages from him already this morning. All apologizing for last night. I didn't know how to feel. I needed to get through today and get my mind into playing at McGlynn's tonight. I just didn't have time for this right now. I'm not even sure I wanted to be in a relationship, and here I was ping-ponging between two men. Worst of all, I hadn't heard a word from Mark.

It was only a few minutes before 8:00 a.m., but there were no open spaces in front of Greene's, so I parked across the street near Shack's. I didn't bother with coffee. I was making myself suffer I guess, wallowing in self-pity by denying myself coffee. The lights were on in Greene's, and the door was unlocked. Carol was busy behind the counter organizing paychecks and grumbling about the general disarray of the office.

She looked up as I came in and said, "I am never taking off again. This place is a wreck! Help me alphabetize these checks before we're overrun with temps."

"What are you doing here?" I scolded. "You're supposed to be resting your back." I paused. "Besides, didn't David fire you? He's not going to be happy to see you here."

"Do you know there was no one here yesterday afternoon?" she asked, ignoring my last comment. "I had five calls on my cell from customers."

Well, that wasn't surprising considering David got his ass kicked by a transvestite. I didn't blame him for not coming back. "How are you feeling?" I asked.

"Better. I just want to get this place in order and get through pay day." She handed me a stack of checks to alphabetize.

We scurried around getting prepared for the rush that would begin at 8:15. I silently prayed it wouldn't be our last one. With the future of Greene's in limbo—not to mention the present—I tried to think positive thoughts that all of the names on the checks in front of me would still be employed next week. Not the least of which, mine.

Before Carol had enacted the Paycheck Pickup Policy, a line of eager temps, their significant others, children, and, on several occasions, pets would be waiting at the front door upon her arrival. I looked out the window as a big, yellow school bus double-parked in front of the office. Traffic screeched to a halt as the stop sign swung out and the red lights flashed. The door opened and a motley group of temps scrambled out.

"Looks like Kenny is right on time today," she commented.

Kenny Jackson was an enterprising young man who worked for Greene's at Harris Manufacturing on the second shift and drove a school bus during the day. After dropping the kids off at school, he stopped at Harris', picked up the night shift temps, and brought them to Greene's to pick up their checks. He made five bucks a person, and the temps were able to pick up their checks earlier than if they had used public transportation. Pretty ingenious. Still, it was a little weird seeing all the temps rolling up to the office in a school bus.

"Hi, Kenny," Carol said handing him a check. "How's the school bus driver business?"

"Can't complain," he said ripping open the envelope and taking a look at his check. "Hey, Miss Carol, have you had any new jobs come in? I'm really lookin' to get off the line and do something else. Man, it just puts me to sleep looking at toothbrushes all night."

Carol nodded sympathetically. "That doesn't sound like fun. But you are probably going to get hired full-time at Harris as soon as they open up some positions. Then you would make more and have benefits," she reminded him.

"Yeah, that's what my mom says, too. But workin' the line is nowhere near as exciting as driving a school bus. I wish I could drive a bus full-time, but it's hard to get into the MTA. I can't even figure out how to complete the online application!" He shook his head. "I'm not that good with computers. We never had one at home. But I know I could pass the driving test."

He looked so earnest that Carol asked, "Can you come by here this afternoon before you have to pick the kids up from school?"

"Sure," he said. "But what for?"

"I'll help you do the online application, and I'll make a call to a friend at MTA."

"Wow," Kenny said, all smiles. "Thanks! I'll be here."

We continued to pass out checks for another thirty minutes until there was a lull. "You're my hero, Carol," I said. "You have the patience of Job, and you go out of your way for people."

"Save the applause," Carol teased. "Happy temps make happy customers. Bored temps get into trouble. Kenny's one of the most reliable people I have working the line at Harris, but he's not going to last much longer staring at toothbrushes. Besides," she added, "the whole online application process makes me crazy. It puts up one more barrier for people who already have the deck stacked against them."

I've heard Carol get upset about the topic of online applications before. She had spent the last twenty years in recruiting and staffing. According to her, ten years ago someone like Kenny would have been a shoo-in for a blue collar job like driving a bus. He could pass the background check, drug screen, the driving test, and had good references. He was a good kid who worked hard and stayed out of trouble. These days, between all the competition for fewer jobs and the laborious online application process, people like Kenny didn't even bother trying to move up in the world. They got stuck looking at toothbrushes for the rest of their lives.

I glanced at the clock. It was almost 9:00. "If you're okay without me I'd like to get an early start with The Count today."

"The Count?" Carol asked. "Oh, Vann. Don't let him hear you call him that. He's pretty touchy about the whole vampire thing," she warned.

I rolled my eyes. "Then he shouldn't wear a cape."

"It's a cloak," said Carol with a straight face.

"You still so owe me for this assignment," I said as I grabbed my coat and purse.

*   *   *

I knocked on The Count's door at 9:10. And waited. I knocked again. This was weird. Finally I heard some rustling behind the door.

"Ms. Hudson," said a disheveled Mr. Pyres in a red bathrobe. "What are you doing here at this infernal hour?"

"Um, it's after 9:00," I said trying to peek around him. "I decided to start a little early to get caught up. Everything okay?"

"I wish you had telephoned first," he said. "I am currently indisposed."

I wrinkled my forehead. "Indisposed?" I repeated. What was this nut talking about?

He jerked his head indicating something in the room behind him. I heard a woman's voice behind him call, "Vanny what's taking so long? The water is getting cold."

Oops! "I am so sorry," I said trying to stifle a giggle. He held up a finger for me to wait and then let the door slam in my face. A minute later he opened the door and stuffed a wad of papers in my hand.

"This should get you started. I'll be down to check on you later," he said.

I couldn't resist. "So I guess this means your date went well?"

He slammed the door in my face again. Really? The Count was getting more action that I was? Well, I consoled myself, it wasn't as if I hadn't had multiple offers this week. I walked down to the office and settled into a workstation. My mind wandered to images of hot, sexy men as the flowery description of fourteenth century eating utensils threatened to put me to sleep. This job had to rival toothbrush inspecting on the boredom scale, I thought, shaking my head to stay awake.

The Count stopped by at 1:00 on his way to lunch with Betty, cape and all. I was actually hoping for a lunch invitation. The prospect of seeing them together would more than compensate for the vegan food. I showed him what I had accomplished so far and told him I would work more over the weekend to get caught up.

"I want to have the manuscript to my publisher next week. The Renaissance Festival is coming up, and I want to be free from work," he said.

Me too. I had a standing gig at the festival. It paid great, and it was fun to dress up as a beautiful maiden for a few days. "I guess there's no need to continue working on the Special Project," I said. Which stunk, because I had been looking forward to the money.

"Oh, on the contrary," said The Count. "It was most successful. We must continue."

"But you already met someone and seem to be hitting it off pretty well," I said looking up at him.

"I think I need to play the field a little," he said with a mischievous smile. "I am having quite a good time with Betty. But I want to keep my options open."

I rolled my eyes. I wondered how Betty would feel about this. "Okay," I said slowly. "I'll work on that when I get back from lunch."

Other than the obvious prostitutes looking for a hook up, there weren't any new prospects. I tweaked a few things on his profile and did a quick search of potential candidates. On a hunch, I looked for women interested in the upcoming Renaissance festival. There were three that looked promising. I jotted off a quick message from The Count about the festival and called it a day.

My phone rang just as I was packing up.

"Hey, have you heard from Mark yet?" asked Carol.

"No. Why?"

"I've had ten more customers that made cash payments to someone identifying himself as the owner of Greene's. I also see that David ran reports of active customers' billing info. I'm worried that he is on the hunt for more cash payments. I tried calling Mark, but it just goes straight to voice mail. I think I should call the police," she said.

"You need to wait for Mark. I don't think the Greene family wants the police involved." I was getting more than a little worried about Mark. What if there had been some kind of altercation in Virginia? David was unstable, and who knew about Marcie's boyfriend? Carol agreed to give Mark until tomorrow. She asked how the Vann Pyres assignment was going. I told her about his big sleepover with Betty.

"I guess there's hope for me yet," she said with a laugh.

"I'm getting pretty good at this online dating thing. Say the word, and I'll hook you up with a profile."

"No thanks," she said. "I prefer to meet my men the old-fashioned way."

"Singing drunk karaoke in a bar?" I jabbed.

"I left myself wide open for that one," she said.

"Don't forget—I'm playing at McGlynn's tonight," I reminded her.

"I'd love to see you play. But there's no way I'm showing my face in that place again anytime soon."

I could see her point.

I left work and went straight home to put fresh strings on my guitar and load the gear in my car. I didn't have a lot to bring because, unlike some places I played, McGlynn's had a decent sound system to plug into. I hated lugging speakers, but since I hadn't made it to rock star status yet, I couldn't afford roadies. My phone rang as I was taking Max for a walk.

"Diana?"

My stomach flipped, and I flushed from my head to my toes. "Is everything okay, Mark?"

"Yes," he said. "Long story. Marcie's not having an affair, but there are major problems with David. I also heard from Ed's accountant. He said that he sent Ed an email over a month ago about the receivable problem. He admits to dropping the ball after that. Doesn't look like there's any funny business on his end."

"At least there's some good news. Carol's been trying to catch up with you," I said and told him about the customers.

"I'm not surprised. Tell Carol to hold tight. I'll catch you both up on everything tomorrow. I still have a few things to take care of here. I'm not sure if I can make it to see you at McGlynn's tonight." He sounded disappointed.

"Not a problem," I said, although I was more than a little disappointed.

"I'm looking forward to our date, Diana. I can't wait to see you."

My stomach flipped again. "I can't wait to smell you either," I said.

He laughed. "That's a little creepy."

"I meant see," I stuttered. I slapped my forehead after we hung up. Sometimes I still felt like a sixteen-year-old klutz.

After calling Carol with an update, I made myself a sandwich and fed Max. He looked annoyed that none of the ham from my sandwich made it into his bowl. I consoled him with a belly rub. I rummaged through my case and pulled out my standard set list for McGlynn's. Over the years I had become skilled at knowing exactly which songs worked at which bars. I played a few chords and ran through a couple of lines from each song to refresh my memory. Nothing worse that forgetting a song on stage.

7:00 p.m. Time to get dressed and go. Now this might come as a surprise, but my performance persona was much more glamorous than the regular me. Bars and restaurants weren't used to having solo female performers and were more than reluctant to hire me when I showed up looking for work in jeans and a T-shirt. This area was more used to older guys in Hawaiian shirts and flip flops singing Jimmy Buffet songs. I found that one of the keys to garnering more gigs was to bring some glam. So out came the high heeled boots, snug black pants, and a shimmering, clingy gold shirt. Big earrings, big hair, and smoky eyes finished my look. It was fun dressing up like a star even if I wasn't one yet.

My phone rang. I checked the number. Oh, great. My mom.

"You're back," I said answering the phone.

"And not a moment too soon," she said dramatically. "Uncle Grover in the hospital, Granddaddy hitch-hiking, you having sex in the back of your sister's van! We leave for a week—one week! And all you do is get into trouble."

I grabbed my forehead. "Did you have a good trip, Mom?"

Distracted from her tirade for a second, she replied, "Yes, but your father threw up for three days straight. Anne was fit to be tied with him."

My dad always threw up on a cruise. Why they kept going on cruises was beyond me. "Sorry to hear that," I said trying to work my way out of the conversation. "I've got a show tonight, Mom. I need to get going."

"Not till I'm done with you," she said. I could picture her straw-colored, over-processed Farrah Faucet hair bouncing around as she tossed her head and pointed her finger at the phone.

"How's Uncle Grover?" I asked to change the subject.

"He's fine. Nice try, but I want to talk to you about this Rick situation."

I sighed. "There's no Rick situation."

"You don't call sex in your sister's van a 'situation'?" she asked.

"We didn't have sex," I replied.

"Because you were interrupted."

Well, she had me there. "What's your point?"

"I think you should give Rick a chance," she said.

I pulled my ear away from the phone and stared at it. "Are you kidding me?" I asked. "You're the one who encouraged me to break up with him in the first place so I could live my life and have some adventures. Remember?"

"That was when you were eighteen. You're on the wrong side of thirty now, Diana. You've sown your wild oats; it's time to grow-up and start a family before it's too late," she said. My mom looks like your classic trailer park mama—think Erin Brockovich without the lawyer smarts—but she has an amazing way of cutting through all the crap and putting her pink and white acrylic nails spot on the truth.

"Rick's a great guy, Mom. No question about that. I'm just not sure about getting serious with him again. We have completely different lifestyles, and I don't think he'd support my music career." It felt good to get those words out in the open.

"What career?" she said harshly. "Wake up, Diana! You're a temp who sings a couple of nights a week at bars. And who's this guy Granddaddy said you were seeing?" Did I mention my mom wasn't warm and fuzzy?

"Mark is just someone I know from work. Nothing serious. Do you have to be so direct, Mom?" I ground out.

"Obviously I do," she said. "I don't want you to miss out on having a real life. A husband. A family. I'm just lookin' out for you girl." Her voice cracked a little. I knew she was saying this for what she thought was my own good, but geez this was too much!

"I have to go."

"Just think about what I said," she replied. "And give Rick a chance. He's our kind of people. He knows you and your family, and he's still interested."

CHAPTER FOURTEEN

———

McGlynn's was still pretty empty when I rolled in with my gear at 8:15. Woody was making small talk with a couple of old guys sipping beer at the bar. "Lady Di in the house," he announced as I approached him. Then he whistled. "Now that's what I call a Queenie Baby."

"Amen," said one of the old guys looking up from his beer.

"Please hold your applause until after I actually sing something," I laughed.

"Your granddaddy isn't coming by, is he?" Woody asked.

"Not a chance! He's at my sister's until at least Monday. Looks a little slow tonight," I said, glancing around.

"Naw, it'll pick up. Queenie Baby always packs the house."

I laughed. "Thanks." It was good to be appreciated.

After a couple of trips to the car, I was ready to start setting up the stage. I was particular about the set-up. If anything was off, my confidence plummeted. I dug around in my guitar case looking for the ever-elusive pick. Inside the case I noticed my growing line of tic marks.

When I first started playing professionally five years ago, I noted each of my performances with a tic mark in the lid of my case. I looked at the long row of marks. I thought about what my mom said as I made a mark for tonight. Was I any closer to realizing my dreams of being a full-time songwriter?

Sure, I had a good following locally, but most of what I did was sing covers. I had a few well-received originals, however, I couldn't make a living off them. Last summer was the closest I had ever come to finding my golden ticket. At the time, I thought I was on my way to the big time. And then nothing. The series didn't get picked up. The producers stopped returning my calls and emails. Should I have taken that as a sign to get a real job and settle down? I wondered.

My mom was right. Rick was definitely the settling down kind of guy. Mark? Who knew? I didn't know him at all. Rick, on the other hand, I had grown up with, experienced all the firsts with. Maybe I was meant to experience other firsts with him like marriage and kids. I found a pick and then dropped it twice before I finally strummed a few notes on my guitar. I had to snap out of this funk.

I ran a couple of sound checks, and then started my set promptly at 9:00. People started to filter in, and a few songs into it John walked in wearing a Hawaiian shirt. He cupped his hands over his face and yelled in his best police voice, "I'm gonna have to cuff you if you already played 'Margaritaville.'"

"Not a chance!" I said over the microphone.

"Darn! I was looking forward to the cuffing part," he called back. The audience laughed, and there were some catcalls from the bar.

I launched into "Margaritaville," and John brought a Margarita over to me. After the song ended, I raised my glass to him sitting out in the audience and took a sip. It was strong. "I think I may need a police escort after that drink," I mugged into the microphone.

I sang a couple more songs and then plugged in my iPod while I took a break and stopped by to see John. "Hey, thanks for coming out," I said, sitting down at the table.

"My pleasure," he said with a big smile. "You're such a wonderful singer, and you look amazing tonight."

He was a sweetheart. Not my type, but a nice guy. "Thank you. Any of your police buddies joining you tonight?"

He shrugged. "A couple said they might stop by," he said. "But I'm happy sitting here watching you all by myself." He leaned his chin on his hand and smiled like a love-sick school boy.

Uh-oh. Better put the brakes on this pronto. "John, you should know that . . ." I began.

"There you are!" a woman's voice yelled from the doorway. We looked up. A short, tiny woman in a frumpy, stained pink sweatshirt and black yoga pants came charging at us. "I followed you. I knew you were up to something!" She was pretty with delicate, almost elfin features. "And here you are!" she said triumphantly. "Hooking up with this floozy!" She pointed at me.

"Hey," I cried standing up. "I'm not a floozy. I'm a singer."

She looked me up and down. "You look like a floozy to me. Husband stealer!" she cried and thunked me on the arm with her short little fingers.

"Ow!" I took a step back, rubbing my arm. "Husband?" I asked looking at John.

John was still staring at me with dreamy eyes. He waved his hand dismissively. "We're separated," he said without even glancing at his wife.

She squawked and, with lightning speed, thunked him in the head.

That seemed to wake him up. "I hate it when you do that, Sheila," he said rubbing his head.

"We're not separated you idiot. Although why I've wasted ten years with you is beyond me," she huffed.

John looked up at me. "We're getting separated," he explained.

She rolled her eyes. "We live in the same house."

"We don't sleep together," John said.

"Because you snore," she shot back.

Time to rescue the situation. "Look, I need to get back to work. But I want you to know that nothing is going on between us," I said to her calmly.

She turned to John. "Tell your Amazon girlfriend that if she doesn't shut up I'm going to climb up on this table and bust her upside the head."

John looked over and gave me an uncomfortable smile. This wasn't going well.

Shelia continued. "I hope you and your Amazon will be happy with each other. By the way," she said addressing me now, "we have four kids under ten, and they aren't coming with me."

I shook my head and started to try to explain one more time. "We're not seeing each other. This is just," suddenly a pair of strong arms wrapped around my waist and pulled me against a hard tall body. Eau de Mark rushed through my nostrils.

"Hi, Baby," he purred nuzzling my neck. "Sorry I missed your first set."

I turned and looked gratefully up at him.

"As I was saying," I said to Sheila, "I have a boyfriend. Mark this is John, a fan of mine, and his wife, Sheila."

John looked crestfallen. Sheila looked like she still had her doubts.

"John has come to a couple of my shows, but there was never anything going on between us," I said again.

Sheila's eyes narrowed. "What? My husband's not good enough for you?" she accused. "You too snooty for a real man? Got to have yourself a Mr. GQ, huh?" She shook her finger up at me, and I moved back a little in case she tried to pluck me again.

Mark tried to stifle a laugh.

She turned on him. "Oh, Mr. GQ thinks this is funny," she snarled. "I guess it's a real hoot to watch a ten-year marriage dissolve right before your eyes." Knowing what was coming, I inched away from Mark. With laser accuracy, she leapt up and thunked Mark square in the forehead.

"Ow," he said clutching his forehead. "What's wrong with you, lady?"

The whole bar was watching at this point. Someone yelled cat fight. This seemed to energize Sheila. She jumped up on the table.

"Jesus, Sheila, get down," John said, finally getting to his feet.

"What's *wrong* with me?" she asked. "I'll tell you! I'm sick of wiping butts and noses all day. Not to mention chauffeuring kids all over town. And now I've got to worry about my idiot husband mooning after some hot-to-trot singer behind my back. Well, I'm done! You can take this job and shove it!"

She paused for a breath and someone hollered, "Tell it sister!"

"I used to be cute," she said starting to tear up. "Now I'm just crusty." She looked down at her stained sweatshirt. I felt bad for her. She did look crusty, and John was an idiot. "But not anymore," she cried as she whipped off the sweatshirt revealing a pink spandex cami that showed off an impressive rack.

A roar went up.

John stared wide-eyed.

Like a stripper at the pole, she threw her sweatshirt into the crowd. "Who wants to buy me a shot?" she yelled climbing down from the table. She brushed past John on her way to the bar without a word.

I looked over at Mark.

"How do you get yourself into these situations?" he asked.

"I did nothing," I insisted.

We both looked at John.

"Guess I owe you an apology," he said sheepishly. "I like you, Diana, but I didn't mean to start all this. I guess things had just gotten a little routine at home." He sighed and looked over at the bar where Sheila was now holding court. "Guess I should go reel her in," he said.

I rolled my eyes. "You think? This was completely not cool."

"Sorry again, Diana," John apologized before he made his way to the bar.

I looked over at Mark, who burst out laughing.

"What are you laughing for Mr. GQ? You've got a big red elf mark on your forehead."

"Pretty nice rack for an elf," he joked looking over at the bar.

I gave him an evil look. "Jerk!"

"Hey," he said, "what did I do? You're the one with married Officer John following you around."

"I didn't know he was married."

"So I'm assuming he isn't hickey guy," he teased.

I glared at him. "No, just a fan."

"Saw some possibility there?" he queried.

"I thought he was a nice guy. That's it," I said. "I need to get back on stage. Can you get me a martini, please?"

"Afraid of going up there yourself?" He looked up at the bar. "She does have a mean pluck," he said rubbing his forehead.

I glared at him and went back on stage and tuned my guitar. He was back in a few minutes with my drink and an update. "Sheila told John he'd better get going because the babysitter needs to go home in fifteen minutes. John asked her to come with him and she said, 'Why? I don't work there anymore'." Mark shook his head. "I think she's going to give him another chance, but right now she's enjoying torturing him."

I didn't care what they did as long as they didn't interrupt my set. I took a sip of my drink. "Ahhh," I purred, "just what I needed." I sighed and looked around the room. It was filling up fast. "Thanks for the save," I said.

"No problem," he said putting his hand over mine. "Again—how do you get in these situations?"

I shrugged. "I have no idea. But I appreciate the bailout."

"I kind of like being referred to as your boyfriend," he said with a grin.

"No comment. I've got to get back up there. Thanks for the drink." Then I turned around and asked, "Mark, do I look like a floozy?"

"Only in the best possible way," he replied.

"Impossible," I muttered as I stomped up on stage. The audience was starting to get antsy. It was time to switch things up. I was feeling the need to let off some steam. I strummed a few unmistakable bars and said into the mike, "Who wants to hear some Lynyrd Skynyrd?"

The applause quieted as I began to sing "Simple Man." I had altered the words a little to make the song work. I looked out over the room and knew I had their attention. There was a certain novelty when a woman sang a traditionally male song. This was one of those songs that made me feel like a rock star. I finished the song to thunderous applause.

"Since you seem to like Skynyrd, how about this?" I said and jumped into "Sweet Home Alabama." Suddenly, the dance floor was full. Even John and the elf-like Sheila, who by this point was too drunk to care about John's indiscretion or the babysitter, were cutting a rug. I watched Mark make his way back to the bar and order a beer. He smiled and gave me a thumbs up. I smiled back. Mark was so comfortable and easy going I sometimes forgot how attracted I was to him. Until, of course, I caught a whiff of him, and then I was like Max with a visitor's leg in his line of sight.

I sang a couple of slow songs to change things up a bit and was happy to see John and Sheila making out on the dance floor. Looks like disaster had been averted there. I glanced at my set list. The end was approaching. I jumped into my original, "The Rum Song," and the dance floor filled up again. A few people were singing along. I looked up at Mark to see if he remembered the song. He was still at the bar. He was talking to a dark-haired man; they both had similar builds. The dark-haired man laughed and looked up from his beer.

Time seemed to stand still. I stumbled over the words.

The man waved to me. It was Rick.

CHAPTER FIFTEEN

———

I don't know how I finished my set, but I did. I quickly thanked the audience and unplugged my guitar. With growing dread, I made my way over to the bar. Mark's face was a mask. Rick jumped off his stool and rushed over to me. He grabbed me around the waist, saying, "You're amazing! You could have knocked me over with a feather when I walked in and saw you up there." He was beaming with pride. I think I had found a new fan. I was thrilled by his reaction despite the complete and utter awkwardness of the moment.

"What are you doing here, Rick?" I asked.

"Trying to make up for being such an ass," he said. "I thought if I came out to see you in action, I might be able to understand where you were coming from."

I glanced over at Mark. Rick's back was to him. Mark could hear every word without Rick seeing him. "You should have let me know you were coming," I began.

He waved that away. "It would have just made you more upset. Besides," he said with genuine excitement, "I finally get why you're so into singing. You've got major talent. You have to pursue this. You were right—I did talk you into majoring in economics, and I'm sorry. I can't even imagine where you would be right now if you had studied music. I'm sorry, Diana."

I saw Mark drop his head in his hands and glance out from between his fingers at me. He shook his head and made the gun to head sign with his fingers. "Rick, I appreciate you telling me this. Truly. But I'm so jazzed up after singing all night that I can't even think right now. I need a drink," I said dropping down on the bar stool.

"Of course," he said. "The bartender's busy. I'll go down to the other end and get his attention."

I could have had Woody's attention in two-seconds flat, but I welcomed the opportunity to set things right with Mark. Staring straight ahead, I said out of the side of my mouth, "I am so sorry! I had no idea he would show up."

I could feel Mark looking at me. "Are you talking to me, lady?"

"Stop that!" I hissed. "You know I'm talking to you."

"What do you expect me to say?" he said with exasperation. "I'm sitting here watching a woman that I'm really starting to get into give an amazing performance, and the next thing I know this guy sits down and says, 'That's my girl up there.' I'm assuming he's hickey guy, correct?"

I glanced over at Rick still trying to get Woody's attention. "Yes," I admitted. "But I'm not his girl."

Mark gave me a 'yeah, right' look. "I didn't think it would be a good time for me to tell him about our date tomorrow. He looks like he could get a little testy given the right motivation."

"He might not like it," I said, "but I doubt he would throw a punch at you."

"Not a risk I'm interested in taking tonight. I've already been plucked in the head by an elf," Mark said wryly. I sat there gloomily wondering why this was happening. As I watched Rick making his way back over with my drink, Mark said, "You know I should rescind my date offer."

I looked over at him quickly.

"Here you are," Rick said. "An extra dry martini. I told the bartender you liked Appletinis, but he insisted you would want this."

I looked up at the bar. Woody gave me a sympathetic nod. I raised my glass to him and downed the drink.

"Whoa, slow down," Rick cautioned. "Not that I would mind carrying you home tonight." He laughed.

I saw Mark pretend to bang his head on the bar.

"Well," said Mark standing, "it was good talking to you Rick. I need to head home." He shook Rick's hand. "That was quite a performance, Diana," he said and shook my hand too.

What to do! I wanted to jump up and run after him. But no way that would work with Rick here. I reached in my purse and quickly typed out a message to Mark:

Me: *I'm so sorry!*

Mark's reply came back quickly.

Mark: *Me too. You two will make beautiful kids together.*

Me: *No! That's not what I want.*

Mark: *What do you want?*

Me: *To go on a date with you tomorrow.*

No answer.

"Who you talking to?" Rick asked, leaning over my shoulder.

"My friend, Carol," I lied smoothly. "She hurt her back at work."

He took a sip of beer. "Too bad," he said. "You ready to get packed up?"

I nodded. "Sure."

"Great," he said, "I'll be your roadie."

I coiled the mike wires while Rick loaded my guitar and a couple heavier pieces of equipment into my car. My phone rang. My sister. Calling at midnight. I don't think so. Probably had a fight with Dan. I ignored the call.

Rick came in looking alarmed. He held out his phone. "It's your sister. She said your Granddaddy was in an accident and is in critical condition at the hospital." I grabbed the phone out of his hand.

"Jesus, Diana, just ignore my call why don't you," she began sarcastically.

"Shut up, Ashley. How's Granddaddy?" I asked.

"Not good," she sobbed. "He's in surgery right now. Collapsed lung. Broken hip. You need to get here right now."

"Okay. We're leaving now." I turned to Rick. My hands were shaking as I handed him back the phone. "Can you drive me to the Dover Hospital?"

He put his arm around me. "Of course. Do you want to leave your car here? What about your dog?" he asked, always the practical one.

Carol would be the only one I trusted with Max, but what to do with my car? No way I could leave all my equipment in it on the street, and I didn't want to take the time to unload at my place. I glanced at my phone. Should I? I hesitated and then called Mark's number.

"I'm still thinkin' about the date," he said abruptly.

"I need help," I said. I told him about Granddaddy. "I need you to get my car, take it back to my place and unload it. Oh, and I need you to take care of Max too." I winced a little at the Max part. That may have been pushing it, but I didn't want to have a dog with me at the hospital. It was going to be enough of a zoo with my whole family there.

"Wow," he said. "You sure know how to treat a guy. I take it you're heading back with Rick?"

"Yes," I said.

"Oh, what the hell," he said. "Go take care of your crazy Granddaddy, and I'll take care of things here."

"Thank you. Thank you. Thank you." I gushed. "You are a life-saver. I'll leave my keys with Woody."

"Ready?" Rick asked after I finished explaining things to Woody.

"Yes," I suddenly felt worried. What if we didn't make it in time. Granddaddy was too old and frail for surgery.

Rick read my thoughts. "Don't get upset. Your Granddaddy is too mean to die."

I laughed. "You're right. He's probably out of surgery and pinching the nurses through their scrubs already."

* * *

Halfway to Dover, I received a message from my sister saying Granddaddy had made it through surgery fine. I relaxed just knowing that he'd made it that far. I shared the good news with Rick, and he gave my hand a squeeze. I glanced over at him. A week ago I could never have dreamed I would be sitting beside him right now. Never. My mom's words rang in my ears. He was "our people," and he accepted my crazy family without question. Of course, he had more than enough cuckoos in his own family tree.

We arrived at the hospital a few minutes before 2:00 in the morning. The alcohol had worn off and left me with a headache. Rick dropped me off at the Emergency entrance and went to park the car. I was much happier facing my family alone. I didn't want the added drama of showing up on Rick's arm.

I could hear them before I could see them. My mom's shrill voice cut through the chatter of the others. "Uncle Grover stop pacing! You're getting on my last nerve."

Then my stepfather, Dave, always the calm, dignified one. "Brandy, dear, don't yell in the middle of the hospital," he scolded.

"Shut up, Dave!" she shouted turning on him. "Granddaddy could be dying right this second, and these sonofabitches won't let us in to see him."

Anne's sobbing reached epic proportions at my mom's words.

I rounded the corner, and they rushed at me. "Oh, thank God," my mom cried.

"Where's Rick?" Ashley asked.

"Hi Mom," I said giving her a hug. "Parking the car," I answered Ashley. "Any news on Granddaddy?"

My dad came over to give me a hug. "They're going to let us in two at a time to see him soon."

Rick came up behind and received a warm welcome from my family. Even in these distressing circumstances, they were still punching the Rick ticket. "What happened?" I asked, taking off my coat.

Uncle Grover fell into my arms and sobbed dramatically, "It's all my fault!"

I stared over his shoulder at The Parents.

"He challenged Granddaddy to a game of chicken," my dad said.

Uncle Grover sniffed loudly. "I challenged him to a duel," he said formally. "However, we couldn't find any weapons so we decided to use lawn tractors."

"What?" I cried incredulously.

The Parents nodded in unison.

"Hacker would have had you, too, if you hadn't cheated and hit him with your cane!" Aunt Pearl yelled, moving towards us as quickly as her walker would take her.

"I didn't hit him with my cane," Uncle Grover insisted. "I was merely defending myself when he tried to push me off."

"Granddaddy was hurt this bad in a lawn mower accident?" I asked.

"No," my dad said between clenched teeth, "he fell off the lawnmower after Grover hit him and then hit his head. Instead of calling for help Uncle Grover stole a car, threw Granddaddy in the backseat, and got into a three-car accident out on Route 13 on his way to the hospital."

I shook my head in disbelief.

Rick said, "Man, you can't make shit like that up."

"That's what the police said," my dad said wryly.

"I didn't steal a car," Uncle Grover insisted. "I commandeered the vehicle in an emergency situation."

"How did he get Granddaddy into the backseat?" I had to ask.

Aunt Pearl raised her hand. "I grabbed his legs and Grover grabbed his arms. My legs might be done for," she said proudly, "but I still got my upper body strength." She curled her arm and pulled back her jacket to show us her muscles. All I saw was a lot of loose skin.

"Impressive," said Rick.

I gave him an elbow to the gut. The last thing The Grands needed was encouragement.

A doctor came into the room and said that Granddaddy was in stable condition. Everything looked good, but he was going to need extensive rehab on his hip.

"Thank God, we put them all at The Meadows," Anne said. "They have an entire wing for rehab."

"If they let him back into The Meadows," my dad reminded her. "He stole their lawn mowers, and then Uncle Grover stole one of the security cars."

"Security car?" Rick said with a whistle. "Did it have the red flashing lights?"

Uncle Grover nodded.

"Cool," Rick said.

I gave him another elbow.

"Ow, stop doing that. Granddaddy's out of danger now. You've got to see the funny side of this."

The Parents gave him a collective evil eye. I think he lost a couple of cool points with that comment.

Anne and my dad went in to see Granddaddy first. "Only a few minutes each," the doctor warned.

Rick and I sat down in a chair. "After you see your Granddaddy, how about getting some sleep at my place? Completely platonic," he added.

Now staying at Rick's sounded so much better than sleeping on Ashley's crud-encrusted couch, but I'm not sure I could live with myself if something 'accidentally' happened at Rick's. "I'll go home with Ashley," I said.

Ashley jumped in. "No, you won't. Dan's sleeping on the couch now. I can't take his snoring anymore."

"Thanks, Ash," I said, "so sisterly of you."

"Seriously, Diana," Rick said earnestly. "Just come to my place. We'll get some sleep, have some breakfast, and then we'll come by here to check on Granddaddy before I take you back home."

I sighed. If this was some cosmic joke, I wasn't laughing. Anne and my dad came out. "He wants to see his Queenie Baby," Dad said.

"Why don't you and Ashley go in next?" my stepmother suggested.

Granddaddy was covered to his neck in white sheets. Monitors and wires ran under the sheets. His ratty gray beard was draped over the top of the covers. He looked like Rip Van Winkle. "There's my girls," he said in a weak voice.

"How are you feeling, Granddaddy?" Ashley asked, softly patting his hand.

"Don't act like I'm dead, girl," he growled.

"Do you remember what happened?" I asked.

"Yep. That fool Grover tried to killed me," he grunted. Then he gave a little smile. "But I guess this makes us even-steven. Hah!"

Great logic. You gave his dog to the SPCA. He almost kills you in a car accident. Sounds even to me. "Let's not worry about all that right now," I said instead.

Granddaddy got riled up. "I want that old coot to come in here and say we're even-steven!" The monitors started to beep and blare. A nurse popped her head in.

"Don't get so upset," Ashley warned him.

"I'll go get Uncle Grover," I said. Good grief!

I went out and told Anne Granddaddy's latest demands. She rolled her eyes and grabbed Uncle Grover's sleeve. "Listen to me, old man," she said in her best retired teacher voice. "You go in there, apologize, and tell him you two are even. Got it?"

For once, Uncle Grover had nothing to say. He nodded meekly.

Rick went out to get the car, and I took the opportunity to text Mark with an update on Granddaddy and to check in on Max.

Me: *Gd is going 2 b ok*

Mark: *Good news!*

Me: *How's it going there?*

Mark: *Made it back here, and we're fine. Max wants to know if he can use your pillow.*

Me: *:) Thanks again.*

I still couldn't believe Mark had agreed to watch my dog and get my car back to my place. He was something else. I said goodbye to my family. My sister came up beside me and put on her coat. "Hey, don't do anything I wouldn't do."

I rolled my eyes at her. "Like you ever do anything," I said with a laugh.

She looked hurt. "I do things."

"Sorry," I replied, "I didn't mean it that way."

"Yes, you did," she shot back. "And you're right. I don't do anything exciting. But at least I get laid on a regular basis." She laughed and said, "See you tomorrow."

CHAPTER SIXTEEN

———

I woke to the smell of coffee. The dark roasted promise lured me from my cozy cocoon. The sun was bright. I reached for my phone. Almost 9:00. Six hours of sleep was a record for me this week. I glanced around Rick's Spartan spare bedroom. No pictures or knickknacks, but the mattress was perfect, and the high thread count sheets were luxurious. Probably his mother's doing. I hadn't noticed much last night as I zombie-walked into the room and fell face down on the bed. I do remember taking the time to change into an old flannel shirt of Rick's before passing out.

My phone rang. I didn't recognize the number, but it was local so I answered it.

"Git me outta here," a mumbled voice demanded.

"Granddaddy?" I asked. "I can barely understand you."

"'Cause they stole my dad-burn teeth," he said. "Now git me outta here!"

"You can't leave until the doctor says it's okay," I soothed. "But I'll be there soon."

I could hear Anne in the background ordering him off the phone. "I need some jerky," he whispered like a junkie to his dealer. "Please, for the love of Pete, bring your Granddaddy some jerky. And don't tell Anne."

I wasn't sure how he was going to eat jerky with no teeth, but I didn't want to disappoint him. "Will do," I promised. "I'll see you in an hour or so."

There was a knock at my door. I glanced around for something else to put on and then thought what the hell. It's not like he hasn't seen me dressed in less before. Rick handed me a steaming cup of coffee with plenty of cream and just a touch of sugar. "You remembered," I said with a smile.

"Of course," he replied. "How'd you sleep?"

"Great! The best sleep I've had in days," I said sipping on the coffee.

"I'm making some breakfast. Any requests?"

"Bacon," I said suddenly starving, "I would love some bacon."

"Wow," he chuckled, "bacon gets you that excited? I may have to trade in my cologne for some bacon grease." He leaned in to grab me around the waist.

This could get dangerous. I dodged him. "Not so fast," I said. "I need to get ready to go to the hospital, and you're making breakfast. No one said anything about any other activities."

He sighed and put his hands up. I grabbed my clothes and purse and headed for the bathroom. Once inside, I leaned against the door. Close one. I was feeling vulnerable, and horny. A bad combination. I glanced around the bathroom. Tiled floor, large glass shower, soaking tub. Sweet. "You've done an amazing job on this place," I called.

"Thanks," he said from the kitchen. "Been working on it nonstop since I got back."

The two-bedroom, one-bath bungalow situated at the back of Rick's parents' potato farm used to belong to the farm manager. When he retired, the Ellises hired a manager who already had a home, so the house sat vacant for a couple of years. I had never been inside before, but it had looked rustic and outdated from the outside.

I put my hair up in a ponytail and took a quick shower. I had enough toiletries in my purse to make me presentable. Too bad I was stuck wearing my clothes from last night. Stage-wear didn't look so great the morning after. The black pants looked fine, but the gold blouse was done for. I put Rick's flannel shirt back on and tied the tails in a knot at my waist. After a swipe of lip gloss and some eyeliner, I was ready to face another day in this wacky week. The smell of bacon wafted through the air as I walked down the short hallway to the combination great room and kitchen. A cheery fire blazed in the large, stone fireplace.

The refinished hardwood floors and pine paneling made me feel like I was in a secluded mountain hideaway instead of four miles from Dover, Delaware.

"That smells wonderful," I said leaning over the breakfast bar and trying to swipe a piece of bacon.

Rick swatted at my hand with the spatula. "Patience," he said and poured me some more coffee.

"I love this place. It is so beautiful."

Rick beamed. "I've enjoyed working on it. It's helped keep my mind off everything." I watched Rick fry the bacon and plate up the eggs. His movements were efficient and graceful. He looked delicious with his wavy dark hair and day-old beard. I could definitely get used to watching him in the kitchen. I had a flash of him without his shirt on leaning over me in my sister's van.

I was feeling a little flushed when he put a plate full of bacon and eggs in front of me. "You okay, Diana?" he asked with a twinkle in his eye. "You look a little feverish."

Just getting hot over you, I wanted to say. But then, of course, I would have ended up flat on my back on one of the very comfy beds. I glanced over at the fireplace. Or maybe in front of…reel it back in, Diana. "I'm fine. Just a little worn out from this week," I said. I dug into my food. Bacon and eggs had never tasted so good.

He nodded in agreement, picking at his plate. "It's been a strange week." He met my eyes for a moment. "But I wouldn't change a thing about it."

I looked down. "When did you learn to cook?"

"Why did you change the subject?"

"Because you're giving me that look," I said.

"What look?"

"You know the one," I said. I crammed in a few more bites of eggs.

He leaned back in his chair. "Are you referring to the 'I'm so happy you're back in my life' look or the 'I want to get you naked' look? 'Cause I think I was giving you both."

I threw my napkin at him and got up to take my plate to the sink. He laughed and grabbed my elbow as I was walking by him. "If you want to talk about looks," he whispered against my ear, "then how about that one you gave me when I was in the kitchen. I think I know which look that was."

I pulled away, scraped my plate off in the trash, and set it in the sink. "Okay, I admit I find you attractive. But that doesn't mean we should just jump into bed together or jump back into a relationship again. There are reasons why we broke up twelve years ago."

"Yeah, I was an asshole. I admit it. I didn't realize how much of one until I saw you sing last night. Give me another chance now that I understand," he said turning on the stool and grabbing my hands. He pulled me in close and tucked his legs around the back of me effectively trapping my body against his. His mouth covered mine, and I moaned against his lips. He had always been a good kisser. Now he was damn amazing.

I pulled myself away. "This can't happen," I said breathlessly.

"Why not?" he whispered against my lips. His warm hands slipped inside the flannel shirt.

I moaned again. He pulled me closer. I was straddling his knees. He reached around and lifted me onto his lap. Face to face with all the good parts lined up just right. My legs involuntarily clinched around his waist. Our lips met again. His tongue penetrated my mouth and sent shivers through my body. He wrapped his arms around me and stood up. He carried me to the couch in front of the fireplace. *Stop this*, my brain shouted. *Not a chance*, my girlie parts shouted back.

"God, I want to be inside you," he growled and nipped at my neck.

Something suddenly clicked. *No hickeys*, my brain shouted. "Stop," I breathed. "I can't."

His lips were on mine again and he murmured, "Give me one good reason why."

I blurted out, "Because I met someone else this week."

His shocked expression was the only warning I got before he dropped me unceremoniously on the couch. "What the hell, Diana!" he shouted, pacing in front of the fireplace. "Who? When? Jesus Christ!" he shouted again and walked out the door in his bare feet.

I held my head in my hands. Why didn't I just go to Ashley's? This was all my fault. Rick was a wonderful person, and I was just leading him on. I guess...but I was so attracted to him. And I could see a future with him. He was ready to settle down, my family loved him, and he had come a long way around to accepting my music career. Honestly, if Mark wasn't in the picture, I wouldn't be so conflicted. Or would I? I wanted to go forward with my life, not rehash an old relationship to try to make it palatable again. Argh!

I glanced out the window. Rick was working off some steam chopping wood. Still in bare feet. My phone started vibrating in my pocket. I pulled it out and checked the number. Now? Really?

"Hi," I said brightly. "How are things going there?"

"Why do you sound weird?" Mark asked.

"I don't," I said keeping one eye on Rick outside. "I mean, I'm not. I'm fine. Going over to see Granddaddy and then home. How's Max doing?"

"Well," Mark said hesitantly. "I've never had a dog before, and Max's communication skills are not so great."

"What happened?" I asked.

"I took him for a walk, but I didn't bring the scooper and bag. He pooped in Mrs. Kester's flowers," he said.

"Oh, no," I winced. "You've got to clean it up. She's going to freak!"

"I'm getting to that part," he said. "So afterwards I came in to get the supplies, and by the time I found everything Mrs. Kester had already found the poop."

"Did she call the police?" I asked.

"No," he said with a chuckle. "She, uh, decorated your car with it."

"What!" I shrieked.

"Calm down," he said. "I'm going to take it through the carwash before you get back."

"So she smeared dog poop all over my car?" I asked incredulously.

"Actually, she wrote I'm going to get you, Diana, and your little dog too!" he said trying to stifle another laugh.

Wow, that must've taken a lot of poop. "I think the old witch is actually crazy," I huffed.

"Well, I think you may have had something to do with that," he said. Then added, "Just a thought."

Good grief. Now I was in a war with the Wicked Witch of the East, or was it West? I glanced up to see Rick walking towards the door with a load of wood.

Better wrap this up. "Well, thanks again. So much. I'm leaving to see Granddaddy in a couple of minutes, and I should be home in the early afternoon. So is our date still on?" I asked as Rick struggled to open the front door.

Mark said, "That depends."

"On what?"

"Any new hickeys?" he asked.

"Nope."

"Any activities that could have led to hickeys?"

"Nope," I said crossing my fingers behind my back. Rick dropped a load of wood in front of the fireplace making a lot of racket.

"I take it he's in the room," Mark said dryly.

"Yep."

I heard some grumbling. "I may be a complete idiot, but let's do this. I'll see you this afternoon," he said and hung up.

I put my phone back in my pocket and looked up at Rick who was busy stacking wood and ignoring me. His feet were still bare and now were more than a little dirty.

"I'm going to take a shower," he announced and headed for the bathroom leaving a trail of footprints.

I wiped up the footprints first, and then I cleaned up the kitchen while he showered. I marveled at how neat and organized everything was. Nothing like my kitchen. I would love to have a beautiful organized kitchen like this, but it would be wasted on me.

Rick came out twenty minutes later looking like he was ready for a photo shoot. Shaved smooth and smelling fabulous. Wow, hard to believe I passed on that this morning. Maybe I would have made a good nun.

He brushed by me and grabbed his coat. "Ready?" was all he said.

I wanted to leave this on better terms. But what could I say? Oh, gee, Rick, if I hadn't met this other complete stranger this week you might have had a chance of getting me naked on your couch this morning.

I decided to try. I put my hand on his arm. "I'm sorry," I said sincerely. "I am just as surprised as you are. I didn't expect this…" I waved my hands ineffectively around and sputtered. "…this situation. I haven't been on an actual date in almost six months. And in one week I've reunited with my sexy ex-boyfriend who appears to have matured a lot faster than I have." I paused, giving him a smile. "And I've met someone else who is completely new to my life and interesting, and I'm attracted to that combination."

"Looks like you're in the catbird seat," he said.

"What's that supposed to mean?"

Rick brushed my hair from my eyes, watching the sunlight catch the golden strands. He said softly, "You let me know when you figure out what you want. I'll be right here."

I sighed and pulled on my jacket. I didn't want to end this on a sad note. God, what a mess!

"Can we stop at the store on our way?" I asked. "I promised to get Granddaddy some beef jerky."

He smiled and patted his coat pocket. "Great minds think alike. I've got his favorite. Homemade deer jerky."

CHAPTER SEVENTEEN

———

The ride to the hospital was quiet. I remarked on some of the changes that had taken place since we used to roam these parts as teenagers. Rick told a few stories of old classmates he had seen since being back in the area.

"I saw Stacey Lynn at the track a couple of weeks ago," he remarked off-handedly.

Immediately my sensors tuned up. Stacey Lynn had been trying to get Rick's attention since junior high. She slept her way through most of the jocks when we were in high school. Rick was the one that got away. We couldn't stand each other.

"I hope she has six kids and stretch marks to match," I said spitefully.

Rick gave me a sideways glance. "Not even close," he said in a tone that indicated how wowed he was by Stacey Lynn. "She doesn't have kids, and she just got back from some type of modeling in Las Vegas."

"Good for her."

"Yeah," he said twisting the knife a little deeper, "we had a couple of drinks. I helped her through some hands of blackjack. We were supposed to go out this weekend, but I cancelled." Rick pulled the car up to the visitors' entrance at the hospital.

"You're a free man, Rick," I huffed, unbuckling my seatbelt and climbing out of the car. "Go ahead and keep your date; I'm sure you will be very happy together." I turned and flew into the hospital. I found the waiting room filled once again with most of my kooky relatives.

"'Bout time you showed up," said Uncle Grover. He leaned in and whispered, "Did you bring the stuff?"

I looked at him like he had lost his mind. "What stuff?" I asked loudly.

He shushed me and took me over to a corner. "Your Granddaddy's stuff? He said you were sneaking some jerky in."

I rolled my eyes. A covert operation for jerky. "Rick has it. He'll be here in a minute."

As soon as Rick entered the room, Uncle Grover pounced on him. "Right this way, Rick. Granddaddy asked to see you two as soon as you got here," he said loudly enough for The Parents to hear.

Annie narrowed her eyes at us. She knew something was up.

Granddaddy was sitting up in bed eating some kind of pudding and flipping channels on the TV. "There's my Queenie Baby. Now where's my stuff?" he asked under his breath.

Rick pulled the bag of jerky out of his coat pocket.

Granddaddy's eyes glowed. "Is that deer jerky?" he asked reverently.

Rick smiled. "Yep, from a deer I got last fall," he said proudly.

"Yee-haa," Granddaddy squealed. "The good stuff. Do you know how much I could get for this down at The Meadows?" He greedily put a piece in his mouth and sucked on it. Which was really all he could do without teeth. "But I wouldn't make a good jerky dealer. I'd be eatin' up all my product," he cackled.

After fifteen minutes of small talk, during which time Granddaddy had to hide his jerky from both the nurses and Anne, we were back out in the waiting room.

"So when does he get out?" I asked my mom who had been eying me since I walked in the door.

"Couple more days and they'll move him to the rehab wing at The Meadows. Probably have to spend a month there," she said looking from me to Rick.

"They're letting him back in The Meadows?" I asked trying to avoid her piercing gaze.

"Your dad found out that Uncle Grover hadn't had his medication in two days. His regular nurse was on vacation, and the substitute didn't have the right orders. The Meadows decided it would be in their best interest to welcome Granddaddy and Uncle Grover back with open arms," she finished. "What's up with you two?" she asked looking from me to Rick.

"Nothing," I said.

Rick just shrugged.

"No," she said, "something happened last night, and not a good something. Jesus, can't you two just get naked and work this thing out."

"Well, I tried, ma'am," Rick said with a smile, "but Diana's being stubborn about the whole thing."

I jabbed Rick in the side. "Get naked, Mom? That's your solution?"

"Well, it couldn't hurt," she said putting her hands on her hips.

"What's all this about getting naked?" my sister asked. She looked me and Rick up and down. "Oh, these two still haven't done it yet? Geez, you're not getting any younger."

I turned to Rick. "Can you take me home now, please?"

"Why are you running off so soon?" my mom asked. "You and Rick should come over to your sister's for dinner tonight."

No, thanks, already got run over by that bus. "I have to get home to take care of Max," I said.

"She has a date with some other guy," Rick said bluntly.

I sucked in my breath and glared at him. "How did you know?"

"Lucky guess," he said.

My mom held up her hands. "Whoa, what's all this about another guy?"

Ashley chimed in. "Someone she met through work."

"What's his name?" my mom asked.

"I'm not talking about this right now," I replied stubbornly.

"The mysterious Mr. X," Ashley laughed.

Rick looked uncomfortable. "I'll go get the car. See you folks later," he said waving to the rest of my family.

My mom eyed me up. "I never took you for a field player," she said. "But I'm impressed. You've got a hot guy like

Rick panting after you, completely besotted, and some new mystery guy you're seeing tonight. Not bad, girl."

"Really, Mom," Ashley said primly. "You shouldn't encourage her."

"Playing the field has a lot of advantages," my mom said to Ashley. "Namely you don't get stuck with the first guy that comes along and tells you you're pretty."

Ashley went red in the face and turned on her heel.

My mom looked at me. "Doesn't mean I'm telling you to take your good ole time with this. You're gettin' a little long in the tooth, and Rick is Dover's most eligible bachelor. He won't be on the market long no matter how he feels about you now."

* * *

Rick politely offered to stop for lunch since it was almost 1:00 as we approached the bridge. I declined, saying I was still full from breakfast. Which was true, but I also didn't want to have to sit and make small talk. I had enjoyed our time together, but now everything felt strained. We pulled up to my condo, and I checked out my car for signs of poop. Thank God, Mark had taken care of that for me. I hoped Rick didn't insist on walking me to the door or, God forbid, coming inside. There was a good chance Mark was still here. I didn't need any more drama.

My phone buzzed, announcing a text message. I pulled it out of my purse.

Mark: *Got Max with me. Didn't want to be there when Rick brought you home. Left you directions to my place.*

I replied: *Thanks!*

Rick cleared his throat.

I looked up guiltily. "Boyfriend number one?" he asked.

"Rick, I am sorry about all this," I began.

He held up a hand. "Don't explain. Just listen," he ordered. "I admit I was pissed this morning. And frustrated by the way you dropped the bomb on our romantic moment."

I tried to say something, and he put his finger on my lips.

"Just listen, please. I'm fine now. I've decided to take the long view with you."

I stared at him. "I don't understand. You're not mad?"

He shook his head. "No, I think the universe is trying to fuck with my head right now. Or maybe it's a test. Whatever." He waved his hand dismissively. "It doesn't matter because I believe that, at the end of all this, we are meant to be together. So go see your Mr. X, and have a good time. Give me a call when you've gotten him out of your system."

I think he had finally lost his mind. "Rick, I don't know what will happen with this other guy. But I'm really not sure that you and I are 'meant to be.'"

"You will be eventually," he said with a smile. "I have faith. Besides I'm not looking to jump back into marriage and all the trappings that go with it right now. My divorce isn't even final yet. So let's both take our time and see what happens."

I looked out the window feeling confused. "I don't know what to say."

He put his hand on mine and raised it to his lips. "How 'bout I just give you a call next week? Maybe I can come over to see you play."

I was still feeling befuddled. The Rick I used to know would have still been pouting or, more likely, yelling about Mark. This new Zen Rick was a little disconcerting. "I play next Saturday at the Pirate's Nest. It's in the Narrows. I'm one of a couple of acts. Some type of biker benefit."

"Sounds like fun," he said easily. "Oh, a word of warning: I don't really know much about it, but I overheard your family making plans to attend the Renaissance Fair. As a group."

"Please, no," I moaned.

He nodded. "They're talking about renting vans."

I looked at him in horror. "The Grands want to see you perform at the Fair. Or as Aunt Pearl said 'I want to see our Queenie Baby play the geetar again before I lay down in the grave.'"

I had a month to talk The Parents out of this idea. I can't even imagine that crew wandering the streets of Annapolis dressed as medieval knights and ladies.

I smiled and leaned over to peck him on the cheek. "Thanks for the intel, and thanks for all your help. I really appreciate it."

His hand caught in my hair and he pulled my lips to his. My toes curled as the kiss deepened. He pulled away first.

"Just because I'm taking the long view about all this, doesn't mean I'm not going to remind you of what you're missing from time to time."

I climbed out of the truck and watched him drive away. For a second I almost waved him back. But I suppressed the urge and headed up the stairs to my condo.

I found generally clean conditions in my condo. A few telltale bacon crumbs on my couch. A couple of dishes in the sink. My bed was neatly made, and the bathroom was spotless. Mark was a stellar house guest. Add in getting dog poop cleaned off your car, and he was a real gem. A slip of paper on the counter listed an address on Dock Street and the instructions:

Head over whenever you can. No heels, dress warm, can't wait to see you.

- Mark

The address was weird. I knew Dock Street like the back of my hand, but I couldn't place it.

What a day already. I decided to take a relaxing bath and wash my hair before going to Mark's. I grabbed a glass of wine on my way to the tub. Hey, it was the weekend, right? I lay in the tub and glanced around the bathroom. Not exactly as luxurious as Rick's, but it worked for me. The condo seemed lonely without Max following me around. He wasn't a snuggly kind of dog, but he loved me in his own way.

It was after 3:00 when I got into my car. I threw my guitar case in the back seat just in case. As directed, I was dressed casually in jeans and suede boots, a long-sleeve T-shirt under a stylish faux-sheepskin vest. It was a beautiful day but a little chilly. The sun was high in the sky as I pulled up to the metered parking area at Dock Street. I grabbed my purse and headed towards the Docks. I kept checking the numbers. The address still didn't look right, I thought, looking at the houses on my left. S23 Dock Street—what kind of address was that? Then I turned my head to the right and noticed the boats. S11, S12, etc.

S23 held an impressive yacht that completely filled the space. On the deck, sitting like the captain of the boat, was Max. He saw me and barked, tail wagging wildly.

"Ahoy, Captain!" I cupped my hands and yelled.

Mark appeared on the deck holding a bottle of wine. "Welcome aboard."

I made my way onto the boat. It was even more impressive up close. It had an old fashioned, well-preserved feel. Opulent even. "Now this is what I call a boat," I said as he helped me up.

"It's Ed's," Mark said with a laugh. "I'm not sure we have the same taste."

"Very old school Hollywood," I said reaching down to pat Max. Max jumped up to give me a hug and wagged his tail appreciatively.

"It probably belonged to some old school movie star. Ed had it completely renovated a decade ago. I think he was trying to impress Marcie, but she can't stand it."

"Speaking of Ed and Marcie...what happened in Virginia?"

Mark sighed, as if his crazy family was the last thing he wanted to talk about now. I could relate.

"I followed Marcie like Ed wanted me to, and it turns out those secretive phone calls she was making were not to a boyfriend."

"Who were they to?"

"Her lawyer. The same place I followed her to. When I confronted her, she admitted that she did put the lease into David's name."

"But why?" I asked.

"Apparently David convinced her he was ready to take on more responsibility. She didn't want to tell Ed until David had a chance to prove himself. She had no idea Ed had sent me here at the same time."

"So, the skimming cash from the business was all David's idea," I mused.

Mark nodded. "It appears so."

"So what now?"

"Ed said he wanted to handle it. That he'd talk to David and set him straight."

I bit my lip. That all sounded well and good, except for the fact that the lease was technically still in David's name. No matter what Ed said to him, Greene's Staffing was still in the hands of a crook.

"You know, I didn't get a hug hello," Mark said, breaking into my thoughts.

He moved in closer, and I was suddenly enveloped in his arms. I breathed in his scent. Heaven. A second later he pulled away and held me at arm's length. He was looking me over carefully.

"What," I asked, "are you doing?"

"Hickey check."

I rolled my eyes but lifted my hair to give him a better look. "Satisfied?"

"Yep," he said pulling me back against him. His lips touched mine gently. "You smell amazing," he said.

"Ditto," I said with a laugh. And then his hands were in my hair, and his lips were hard on mine. He trapped me against his body. My stomach flipped, my heart fluttered, I leaned in closer.

He pulled away. "We need to get going," he said. "I have a surprise."

I would have happily continued to make out on the deck, but I loved a surprise. "We're taking this thing out?" I asked, looking around for a crew.

He laughed. "It's not that big. I brought it up here by myself. Come on in and take a look around."

"If you say so," I said.

He was right. All the nautical gear looked very modern despite the polished oak and brass trimmings. There was a living/dining room with a table for four, a small galley-style kitchen, and an impressive master bedroom with a king-sized bed and master bathroom. The bed looked super comfy. The kind you could roll all around and get lost in.

"Nice bed," I said.

"It sure is," he replied with a wicked grin. "Want to try it out?"

I cut my eyes at him. "We'll see."

He laughed and grabbed my hand. He led me back up to the deck. "We have to untie the boat. Can you get that side, and I'll get this side?"

"I'll give it a try." Despite living near the water most of my life, I didn't have a lot of experience with boats. Especially boats like this.

A few minutes later, Mark fired up the engine. I stood next to him as he carefully maneuvered the boat from the slip. We headed down the inlet towards the bay. The sun was low on the horizon to our right.

"Where are we going?" I asked.

He leaned over and said softly against my ear, "Off into the sunset."

CHAPTER EIGHTEEN

——

We had the bottle of wine and a tray of fruits and cheeses on the deck. Mark had set up a table in front of rattan deck furniture, complete with pillows and a blanket for the chill. We were anchored off Thomas Point State Park, located within a few miles of the Chesapeake Bay Bridge. He had perfect timing, I thought, as I sipped wine and watched the sun approach the horizon.

"I'm impressed," I said clicking my glass to his and waving in the direction of the setting sun. "How did you pull this off?"

He shrugged. "I checked the weather today and saw how calm and clear it was supposed to be. Believe me, you wouldn't be so impressed if the wind was blowing right now. But I'll take the compliment," he said patting my leg.

Max took that to mean that he was wanted up on the sofa with us. Mark looked down at him. Max looked from Mark to me as if to say, "What's his problem?" I laughed and grabbed the blanket, tucking it around us. Mark poured some more wine and offered me the fruit and cheese platter. Max was tempted to beg, but he knew that would end his furniture-time. He curled up on the blanket with a sigh.

"I swear I can hear what that dog is thinking." Mark laughed and scratched Max's head. Max flipped over for a belly rub instead.

"Yeah," I agreed, "he has a way of making himself heard without a sound."

Mark leaned over and kissed me lightly. "This light suits you. You look like a golden mermaid." He played with the ends of my hair. Max growled. "Guess he doesn't like me kissing you," he said looking down at Max.

"No," I said, "you stopped rubbing his belly." I pulled the blanket over Max's head. He didn't protest. "So what else do you have on the agenda for tonight?"

"I thought we would cook dinner together," he said. "I bought some fresh rockfish today, maybe put it over pasta or rice?"

"Sounds wonderful. I love fresh rockfish." Cooking in the close quarters of the galley kitchen located tantalizingly close to the big bed could get interesting, I thought, as the wine relaxed me and the evening's possibilities stretched before me.

"Could we get something out of the way?" he asked.

I tore myself away from visions of the big bed and faced him. He sounded serious. "Sure," I said taking a gulp of wine.

"Where do things stand between you and Rick?" he asked turning to face me.

"I don't know," I said honestly, returning his look. "Yes, I stayed at his house last night. I slept in the spare room. But I will admit there is still an attraction. I can't help thinking about what might have been. I also have my family telling me how wonderful he is and that I shouldn't miss my chance with him again." I sighed. Why did I have to have this conversation now? All I wanted was to watch the sun set and climb in that big bed.

"So where's that leave us?" he asked.

Might as well just rip the Band-Aid off. "I don't know you. But I know Rick. Yes, he's matured and changed for the better. He seems genuinely supportive of my career now. If he was like this twelve years ago, we would never have broken up. But I'm not sure that would have been best for me. My family wants me to settle down. Rick is definitely ready to settle down with me."

"What do you want?" Mark asked.

Interesting question. What did I want? "Well, I'm not ready to settle down yet. I don't want to move back to Dover. I don't want a real job—whatever that is," I said searching my heart for the truth.

"What do you want?"

"I want to live in my little condo, play music, eventually sell some songs," I paused and looked up at him. "And I want to get to know you."

"Good," he said. "I want that, too." He reached for my hands and pulled me to my feet. He wrapped his arms around me. I leaned my cheek against his rough wool sweater that smelled so divine. I raised my lips to meet his. Softly kissing him at first, and then I ran my tongue over his lips. He gave a little growl and pulled me closer. I felt him hard against me, and I rubbed provocatively against him. He bit at my lip and said, "You keep that up, and we'll be rolling around on the deck."

I laughed. "I was thinking more about that big bed below deck."

"You like my big bed, huh?" he whispered against my ear.

I felt a flush that was a tantalizing mixture of wine and desire spread through my body. The sun was sliding into the horizon, and a chill breeze ruffled my hair. "Yes," I murmured and kissed him again.

He pulled away first. He held me at arm's length. "Just one more thing," he said earnestly. "During this getting to know me phase, Rick is out of the picture, right?"

That gave me pause. "I'm not with Rick, so I don't see how I'm supposed to break it off with him, if that's what you're asking." I had no desire to deal with that ugly scene or with the fallout from my family.

"Rick is in love with you," Mark said. "He thinks that once he proves himself to you, that you two will be together."

True, I thought.

"You have to tell him that isn't going to happen, or he's just going to keep trying."

"I'm not sure that would deter him," I said, thinking back to our conversation this afternoon.

Mark pulled back a little more. "Look," he said with a sigh. "As crazy as I am for you, I'm not going to be the odd guy out like I was at the bar last night. I felt like your husband had walked in on our illicit rendezvous. Ten years ago I probably would have cared less, and I know we would've already been trying out the big bed by now. But I don't want that anymore."

"You're right. I don't want that either. I handled that all wrong." I looked at the deck.

"So," he prompted.

"So," I said slowly, "I'll tell Rick that my date went great and that I'm seeing you. Exclusively." That was going to be a tough conversation. I didn't want to hurt Rick, but I couldn't deny my desire to be with Mark. Rick was comfortable and familiar. Mark was just as comfortable, but so much more exciting. I wanted to get to know him, have adventures with him…fall in love with him. He pulled me in closer, and I tilted my face up for a kiss.

A few minutes later, we were getting carried away again. The deck was starting to look like a good option. A scratch on the leg and a loud bark broke the spell. Max looked up at us and whined.

"What's his problem?" Mark asked, pulling away reluctantly.

"Uh-oh. I know that look," I said. It was the 'I've got to poop look.' "Don't suppose you have a dog park on board?"

"Nope," Mark said. "I guess I didn't think this through. Can he go on the toilet or could we hold him over the side?"

Max and I looked at Mark like he was crazy. "Geez, you really know nothing about dogs."

"How about a box?" he asked. "You know like a cat uses. I probably could find a box."

"I don't think a box would work," I said. Max whined again. "Could we head to shore?"

"I guess I could move closer to shore and then take him over in the dingy," he said staring longingly at my lips.

I had a life-sized picture of Max and Mark being lost at sea in the dingy. "Maybe we should head back to the dock. I'm not sure how he would do in the dingy. I hate to ruin your plans," I said, leaning up to kiss him.

"No worries," he said and pulled me against him. "The bed works fine no matter where the boat is."

Another whine from Max settled it. I watched the orange and pink horizon where the sun had been as Mark pulled up the anchor and started the engine. "Thanks for interrupting my romantic date," I said shaking my finger at Max. "You had better go when we get back." Max's tail drooped, and he skulked back into the cabin.

*   *   *

After some cussing and coaxing, Max finally did his business. I'd left Mark at the boat to get started on dinner while I searched out a spot for Max on Dock Street. On my way back, I stopped by my car and grabbed my guitar. The smell of rockfish seasoned with Old Bay greeted me as I climbed onboard. Max sniffed appreciatively.

"None for you," I said sternly. Luckily, Mark had thought to bring Max's food.

"Smells delicious," I said, walking down the narrow stairs into the galley kitchen.

"Me or the rockfish?" he asked, stirring something on the stove.

I laughed. "Both. How's it going?" I asked and kissed him lightly.

He put down his spoon and pulled me against him. "Not so fast," he said and kissed me again with feeling.

Max scratched at his leg.

"Not again," he moaned.

"No," I said, "I think he wants to eat now."

"Geez, it's like having a kid," he complained.

"Tell me about it," I said, digging around for his bowl and food.

Max had nothing to say. He was hungry, and we were his servants. Simple.

"I need more wine," Mark said.

"I'll make myself useful and open a bottle. You look like you're doing great in the kitchen. I wouldn't want to wreck it." There was an impressive wine cooler in the spacious living/dining area. I uncorked a bottle of expensive looking white.

I handed Mark his glass.

"I see you brought your guitar. Why don't you serenade me while I finish up in here?" he asked.

"Sure. Any requests?"

"Something original," he replied.

"I've got just the thing." I carried my wine back into the dining area and took out my guitar. I pulled a chair up to the galley entrance and strummed a few notes. I fiddled with the tuner. "I wrote this about the Chesapeake Bay," I said and launched into the sweet, melodic song that sounded like something John Denver would sing. The song reminded me of warm summer days spent playing outdoors on little decks and patios around town. Every bar and restaurant wanted to be able to boast outside seating and live music during the busy tourist season.

"I loved that," Mark called from the kitchen. "That must go over great around here."

"Yeah, I get a lot of requests from locals for that one," I said. "Let's try something more upbeat." I sang a couple of Jack Johnson songs, and then Mark announced dinner was ready.

We ate by candlelight at the heavy oak dining table. The rockfish was amazing, the conversation stimulating, and the sexual tension was building. "Delicious," I purred and sipped some more wine. I had just enough buzz on to make everything soft and fuzzy.

He took my hand and kissed the palm and then the wrist. I sucked in my breath. "You," he said, working his way to the inside of my arm with his lips, "are delicious."

His lips sent shivers down my arm and a fever through my body. All the good parts were in overdrive.

Max barked. "Shut up, Max," I yelled. Then I heard it.

"Yoo-hoo," a girly voice called down the stairs. "Are you down there, Mark? Come out, come out, wherever you are." She sounded drunk and overly friendly. I heard her heels clicking on the stairs before I saw her.

Mark was out of his chair and moving to head her off. "Megan," he called. "I'll be right up."

"No," she said coming down the stairs. "I'm coming into your lair." She looked like she had walked off of the *Jersey Shore* set. Dark, straight hair, over-done eye makeup, big boobs in too small a dress. "Oh," she said looking at me, "I see you have company. Guess I should have called first."

Mark ran a hand through his hair. "What are you doing here, Megan?" he asked.

"Well, Daddy had business here, so I tagged along for the ride. I saw your boat when we pulled in. It's been months since I've heard from you," she scolded.

"I've been in Atlanta, and there was no reason for you to hear from me," Mark said.

"Oh, Mark, you can't still be mad about what happened last summer. I was silly and young then."

"I'm fine with last summer. But I'm not happy about right now," Mark ground out. "You need to go."

"Oh, whatever," she huffed. "You always were such a square. I don't know why I ever gave you the time of day." She flipped around and headed for the stairs. She paused and shot me a nasty look. "That bed's not as comfortable as it looks, sweetheart."

I smiled and gave her the finger. Max growled at her. She acted like she was going to come down the stairs after me, but she ran into Mark's chest. "Go," he ordered, following her to make sure she did.

I heard some more squabbling up on deck, and then there was silence. I poured more wine. Maybe I should just get drunk. Max leaned against my leg in sympathy.

Mark came down the stairs. "I'm so sorry," he began.

I held up my hand. "Hey, I'll be the last one to throw stones in this situation. She looks like a lively one," I added with just a little snark.

"That was during my Jack Daniel's summer, as I fondly call it." He shook his head ruefully. "I'm not proud of it. And I only saw her for a couple of weeks."

I stood up and started clearing away the dishes. "I guess we've all had those kinds of summers," I said thinking back to last summer. I worked at cleaning up the kitchen while Mark finished in the dining room. Things were a little tense. The date had taken a wrong turn, and I wasn't sure it was going to get back on track tonight.

Mark came up behind me and put a stack of dishes in the sink. "Don't worry about all this," he said indicating the messy kitchen. "I'll take care of this later."

"No. You cooked, I'll clean."

I finished up a few minutes later and found him sitting on the over-stuffed couch drinking what looked like a Jack and coke. I took the glass from his hand without a word and took a swig. Nope it was rum. I sat down on his lap and handed him back his drink. I leaned into his broad chest. The rough wool sweater he had worn outside was gone and replaced by a soft navy T-shirt.

"I guess this means you're not pissed about Megan," he said hopefully.

"Well, you have to admit it was pretty bad timing. But, like I said. I know how things like this can happen because they always seem to happen to me. So no hard feelings." I snuggled back against him and pulled his arms around my waist. It was hard to believe that I hadn't known him even a week yet. He was so easy to be with. I heard his phone buzz. He ignored it.

He put his drink down on the end table. His lips found the back of my neck. "You are the most amazing woman, Diana," he murmured. His lips on my neck sparked an immediate reaction down below. Engines were roaring back to life. He lifted my hair over my shoulder and ran his tongue over the back of my neck. I gave a little groan. "You even taste as good as you look. I can't wait to taste the rest of you."

I flipped around and straddled him on the couch. My lips hungrily connected with his. Just the thought of his lips down there made me crazy. Off came my vest as his hands worked their way under my shirt and lifted it smoothly over my head. His hands found my breasts, and it was his turn to groan. His hands dropped to my rear and scooped me up to flip me backwards onto the couch. My mind briefly thought about this morning on Rick's couch before Mark's kisses and hands blotted out everything else. My jeans were gone in a flash. He stood up to take off his shirt. Wow, he looked amazing without his shirt on. I had to touch him. I jumped up and pressed my hands against his chest. He wrapped his hands in my hair and pulled my head back, so he could put his lips to my neck.

"Go ahead," I said impulsively in response to the light suction from his lips.

"I don't need to," he whispered against my neck. "I've got nothing to prove."

"I want you to," I said not really knowing why.

"Okay," he said with a wicked grin, "but I know a better place."

CHAPTER NINETEEN

———

His hands deftly removed my bra, and I shimmied out of my panties. He drew me back down to the couch, and I laid there naked as he watched me. A few seconds ticked by. "You are so gorgeous," he said starting to pull down his jeans.

I heard a horn beep once, then twice. Max started barking. Mark's phone buzzed again. "Jesus," he said, "this wouldn't be happening if we were still anchored in the middle of the bay."

He grabbed his phone and looked at the number. "Shit," he swore softly. The beeping started again.

"Another girlfriend from the Jack Daniel's summer?" I asked, pulling a blanket around me from off the back of the couch.

He ran his hand through his hair. "No," he said, "it's Ed."

"So call him back. And then get back over here," I added, making grabby hands at him.

"Not that simple," he said. "I'm pretty sure that's him beeping out there."

"He's here?" I cried. "Now?"

Mark nodded. "Yep. I'll go out and talk to him. You stay right there." He leaned over and kissed me soundly on the lips and copped a feel while he was there. I swatted him away playfully.

"Just hurry back," I pouted. "My engine is revved up and ready to go."

I could hear his phone buzz again as he made his way up the stairs. I leaned back on the couch and pulled the blanket more tightly around me. As my body started to cool, I found the voice of reason edging back in. Maybe this wasn't such a good idea. After all, I hadn't talked to Rick yet. And this was technically our first date. I chewed my cuticle and mulled the situation over, hoping that Mark would be back soon and make me forget all these doubts. To pass the time, I checked my phone. Five missed calls! What the heck?

It was Carol. The phone rang twice before she picked up. "Where are you?" she snapped.

"Uh, I'm sort of indisposed," I said.

There was silence on the other end.

"Are you naked?" she asked.

"No," I said hugging the blanket to my chest. Man, did she have X-ray vision or what? "What's wrong?" I asked.

"I've been trying to reach you or Mark for the last three hours," she said. "Wait. Is he there naked too?"

"No. I mean, yes, but we're not naked!" I said with exasperation. "Just out of curiosity, why do you think we're naked?"

"Temps call me all the time from the bedroom, bathtub, and even the toilet. I know when people are naked on the other end of the phone, and you sound like you're naked."

I was impressed. Carol could hear naked. Who would have thought it? "Again, what's going on?" I asked impatiently.

"I decided to go into the office and try to get caught up. I was back in my office, and I had the door closed. All the other lights were out. I heard two men come in and have a conversation. I peeked out and saw David and an older guy. They were talking about getting the information to a guy named Doug down in Miami," she paused to take a breath, and I took the opportunity to fasten up my bra. It seemed obvious to me that naked time was over. "Anyway, the older guy said, 'This will give us enough to start over someplace warmer.' Here's the thing: David called him Dad! After they left I checked any recently accessed files on the computer. It was the temporary employee payroll info. Everything is in there—Social Security numbers, birthdates, addresses."

"Oh, no," I said, the implications of this sinking in. Not only was David skimming cash, he was also an identify thief! "How many employees?"

"All of them," she said. "Over six thousand records."

"Six thousand?" I asked with surprise.

"It's everyone who's ever registered with Greene's since we opened thirty years ago. This is major. When I couldn't reach you or Mark I called Mr. Greene direct and got through. When I told Mr. Greene about David calling the guy 'Dad,' I heard Marcie break down in the background. From what I could tell between her sobbing and Ed's yelling is that David's long-lost father is back in town. And he's not a nice guy. Mr. Greene said he was on his way here and would be in around 9:00."

Great. Just great. "He's here at the boat slip," I said with a sigh.

"Ooh, you're on the boat. It's something else, isn't it? I was on it when Mr. Greene was in town for the boat show a couple of years ago," Carol gushed. "Very romantic."

"Yeah, it was," I muttered. I disconnected and pulled my shirt over my head.

Mark came down the stairs in his bare feet looking deliciously tousled. "Darn," he said with disappointment. "I was hoping to catch you still naked. I have this vision of you stretched out naked on the coach burned into my retinas."

"Highly unlikely considering everything that's going on. Carol just called," I said struggling into my jeans. Not as sexy getting back into your clothes as it is getting out of them.

Mark stopped my hands from buttoning my jeans. "A guy can wish," he said and kissed me like we had all the time in the world.

I pulled away. "Ed's still outside?"

Mark grabbed my hips and pulled me against him. "Yep. He's waiting in his car."

"Then we'd better get going," I said pulling away. "You're only going to get me more frustrated."

He laughed. "Bet you've never had foreplay like this before."

I rolled my eyes. "You have quite the technique."

* * *

Ed's car turned out to be a limo. Max sat curled up on the plush upholstery next to me. He seemed to be accustomed to limo rides. Made me wonder who had owned him before I picked him up from the pound. I was less comfortable. I was the one-person audience at this family drama, and I was sure nobody was happy about airing their dirty laundry in front of me.

Marcie was beside herself with worry. She barely acknowledged my presence. "This is all my fault, Eddie," she sobbed. "I should have told you straight-away that Charles was back in town. I thought I could handle it. I only wanted to help David."

From what I could gather from the conversation, Charles had shown up looking for David about six months ago. Marcie had been horrified that her grifter ex was trying to worm his way back into David's life. She spent months trying to persuade David to stay away from his father. When David brought up running the staffing agency in Annapolis, she had latched on to the idea as a way of getting David away from his father. But it wasn't until Mark confronted Marcie about the missing money that she realized it was Charles who had orchestrated the whole deal in the first place. He had been working on this con game since last year.

"No, Marcie," Ed said, "it's my fault for not paying closer attention to the business. I just don't have the time or the interest anymore. This wouldn't have happened ten years ago. Now we have thousands of employees' personal information in the hands of a con man. And David set up to take the fall."

Ed was in a tough position. Go to the police, and they'd arrest David for sure. Charles was clever and probably had multiple aliases. He might get away, leaving David to take the full rap. These were Federal crimes. Even with the best lawyers David was looking at years in a Federal prison. On the other hand, if Ed didn't report the theft soon, he would be responsible and could face civil and criminal penalties. The clock was ticking.

I glanced over at Mark. He appeared deep in thought. He squeezed my hand and looked over at me. "Sorry about our date," he said softly.

I shrugged. "It's been a night to remember so far," I said quietly back.

Marcie's phone rang. "David!" she exclaimed. "Baby, where are you? NO! You can't leave without seeing me." She paused and covered the phone. "What do I do Eddie?" she whispered furiously.

"Offer him money," Mark said bluntly.

Marcie narrowed her eyes at him. "You shut up. This is all your fault! Always sucking up to Ed."

Ed held up his hand. "Offer him money, Marcie. Tell him to meet you at the bar across the street from Greene's—McGlynn's—in an hour. Promise to come alone."

Marcie relayed the information. "I can bring ten," she glanced hesitantly at Ed who gave the up sign with his thumb, "no, twenty-thousand in cash. Okay, baby, I'll see you soon."

She hung up the phone and sobbed on Ed's shoulder. Poor Ed. May-December love was tough.

We pulled up to Greene's, but I didn't see any lights on. We exited the limo and moved silently up to the door. Ed dug out a large key ring. "I remember the first time I ever opened this door with my own key," he said, his voice gruff with emotion. "Thirty years ago. A lifetime."

We all piled in behind Ed. The blinds were drawn tightly across the windows. Carol opened the door to her office, and light flooded the dim room. "Thank God, you're here," she said rushing out.

Ed offered her his hand. "It's been too long, Carol."

She shook it. "Definitely, Mr. Greene. I'm sorry about this. I guess I wasn't keeping as close of an eye on everything as I should have," she apologized.

"Nope," Ed replied. "I haven't been doing my job as the owner. You remember, Marcie," he said indicating his wife.

Carol smiled and nodded.

Marcie said, "What are we doing wasting time here, Ed? Get me the money and I'll go over to the bar."

I glanced over at Mark. He looked ready to explode.

Ed said, "We need a plan. I'm not just handing David and his dead-beat father twenty-thousand in cash and waving good-bye to them. We have to convince David to turn Charles in."

"Fat chance," said Mark. "No way David is turning in his father. David thinks this is his big chance to make it on his own. We have to get the information back and confirm they haven't copied it or transmitted it somehow," Mark said.

"They talked about going to Miami with the data to get paid. I doubt they would transmit it before they received the money," Carol reasoned.

"Shut up, all of you! I need to get over to the bar," Marcie cried. "If I can just talk to him face to face, I know I can make him understand."

Ed turned to Marcie. "You're ready to tell him the truth about what happened ten years ago?" he asked.

She nodded and wiped her eyes with a tissue. "I should have done it years ago. None of this would have ever happened."

Ed pulled her to him and patted her back. She sobbed noisily against his shoulder.

"What's this big truth?" Mark asked with enough sarcasm to warrant a black look from Marcie.

"Might as well get it out in the open, Marcie," Ed said softly.

I leaned forward. This was better than any reality show on TV. Marcie took a deep breath and looked defiantly at her audience. "I was young and dumb when I met Charles and had David. I used to help Charles in his cons. I guess you could call us professional grifters," she shrugged and added, "only we weren't that good. Charles ended up in prison when David was five and stayed there for ten years. He heard about Ed through some temps that had ended up in prison. Everyone in Annapolis had heard about Ed's rags to riches story—from small staffing firm owner to multi-millionaire real estate tycoon. Ed was a mark in Charles' con game. He wanted me to feather our nest for when he got out."

"I knew you were a conniving bitch," Mark growled.

Ed held up his hand. "No, Mark," he said. "You have to hear the whole story."

Mark ran his hands through his hair and clenched his jaw. I put my hand on his. Things were getting tense.

Marcie continued, "I didn't want any part of it. I had been raising David and working as a secretary in a little law firm outside of DC. I had been hoping that Charles had changed in prison. He put on a good show when I visited him every week, but he insisted I never bring David. When I told him I wasn't going back to working cons with him, he said that if I didn't help him he would take David and run." She broke down sobbing. "So I did it. I quit my job and moved to Annapolis. I signed up at Greene's staffing and managed to bump into Ed on as many occasions as possible."

Ed smiled wryly. "Marcie is pretty hard to forget once you've bumped into her a few times. I was smitten. I had worked hard for so many years that I thought I had missed the chance to have a family. In Marcie and David I saw that chance again."

Marcie cut in. "Once I saw Ed with David, I knew I couldn't do what Charles wanted. Two days before Charles was scheduled to get out of prison, I went to him and told him the con was off. He said that I should say goodbye to David. I didn't know what to do, so I went to Ed and told him everything," she said, glancing up at Ed.

"Tough pill to swallow," Ed said. "But I believed her and wanted to protect David. When Charles got out I met him at the prison gate with a suitcase full of money. 'Congratulations,' I said, 'your con worked like a charm. Now take the money and run.' He never said a word—just opened the suitcase, looked inside, closed it back up, and walked away. Forever we had hoped."

Mark shook his head. "I can't believe I am just hearing this for the first time. And David has no clue?" he asked.

Marcie shook her head.

"Okay, let's give Marcie some time with David. This story might just convince him to wait before heading to Miami with Charles. We can't just go in there. David will see us and run."

"He's never met Carol yet," I said.

Carol shot me a look. Maybe I shouldn't have volunteered her.

Mark turned to her. "I know it's a lot to ask, but if you could sit at a table nearby and feed us info on how it's going, this might just work. If it looks like he's going to bolt, then we'll meet him at the door," he said, indicating Ed. "Threaten to call the police and turn Charles in."

"If it comes to that, I'll buy the data back from Charles. Whatever the cost," Ed said grimly.

"And have the guy come back every couple of years trying to shake you down?" Mark asked with exasperation. "No, this has to end now."

Ed shook his head. "Not until David is out of trouble. Then I'll spend every last dime I have hunting Charles down and making sure he can't do this to me or anybody else again."

CHAPTER TWENTY

———

It was 9:40 when Carol went across the street to stake out a seat at McGlynn's. It was a busy Saturday night. We were betting that Woody wouldn't see her and blow her cover. From an empty office on the second floor, we watched Marcie cross the street a few minutes later. Once David was inside, Mark and Ed would wait outside of McGlynn's in case David bolted. I would keep a watch on McGlynn's and stay on the phone with Carol and Mark in a three-way conference. I felt like I was in a James Bond movie. I understood why they didn't want to call the police, but geez, this was quite an operation. We watched a couple of people walking towards McGlynn's. Ed pointed out David.

Mark gave me a quick kiss on the lips. "Don't say I didn't take you anyplace on our first date," he joked.

"Yeah, this is some date." I paused. "Be safe. This doesn't seem like much of a plan."

I let Carol know it was a go and that Mark and Ed were in position. She was ordering a drink and mumbling out of the corner of her mouth into the phone. "He's sitting down, he's angry."

I interrupted. "You need to pretend like you're talking to someone not like you're wearing a wire," I said.

"Oh, yeah. This is so crazy. I can't believe you volunteered me for this," she whispered furiously.

"Well, I guess this makes us even for the vampire assignment," I said trying to keep things light. And no sooner were the words out of my mouth, when a jaunty red cape caught my eye a block away. "Oh, no," I said into the phone. "He's here."

"Who?" Carol and Mark both asked. I had forgotten about Mark.

"The vampire," I said.

"What?" Mark asked.

"Mr. Pyres is coming in here?" Carol asked in alarm.

I watched him stop in front of McGlynn's just a few feet from where Ed and Mark were standing. He said something to the woman on his arm and held open the door for her.

"Yes!" I said, and heard Ed ask Mark if capes were coming back in style. "Go to the bathroom or something," I yelled into the phone.

"I can't. Something's going on with Marcie and David. She's crying. He's pounding his fist on the table. Wants to know where the money is…" Carol trailed off, and then I heard him.

"Good evening, Miss Smith," drawled The Count. "So lovely to run into you this evening. I must introduce my date, Miss Getty."

Carol must have put the phone down on the table.

"Betty, Carol is the manager of Greene's staffing right across the street."

I was sure every eye in the place was on the guy in the cape. Hopefully, David was too involved in his conversation to notice.

Carol greeted Betty, and I heard Mr. Pyres loudly recount his experiences with Greene's Staffing and Carol. I heard someone, presumably David, shout, "Carol from Greene's! What's this, some kind of set-up, Mom?"

Mark said, "Should we go in?"

"Give her a minute," I replied.

"Do I know you?" Carol asked smoothly.

I heard David curse and knock a chair over.

Mr. Pyres asked, "Is something amiss, Miss Smith? Do you require assistance?"

"I can't believe you'd think for a minute that I would want to run that place, Mom! It's full of freaks and weirdos. Just look at this nut!" David yelled.

"I beg your pardon, sir," huffed The Count. "There is no need to be insulting."

"You know exactly who I am, lady," David said to Carol, ignoring Mr. Pyres. "Obviously, my deluded mother has roped you into her little scheme."

"I'm sorry," Carol replied. "I don't believe we've met."

"No?" he asked snidely. "Well, I know you. You're the one that's been helping my asshole cousin pin everything on me and my dad. Don't think we'll forget it."

"David!" I heard Marcie shriek.

"Shut up, Mom," David growled. "I don't believe any of your story. Dad said you'd try something like this."

"I must insist you refrain from speaking to ladies in this manner, sir," Mr. Pyres said formally.

"Or what? Are you going to bite me?" David said sarcastically.

There was a loud noise and then a thump. I watched as Mark and Ed raced inside McGlynn's. There was shouting, and then the line went dead. Max started barking ferociously. The hair on his back stood up making him look like a white, fluffy porcupine. His lips curled over his crooked overbite and he growled in a tone that I hadn't heard before. I spun around. At the door stood an older, rougher version of David.

"You must be David's father," I said.

"Put the phone down," he replied.

"What are you going to do if I don't?" I asked, buying time so I could hit 911.

He pulled something out of his pocket.

"Is that a gun?" I asked. I had no real experience with guns, but it didn't really look like one.

"No, it's a Taser. Drop the phone. Now!" he yelled.

I hesitated. I didn't want to get Tased, but I figured I could probably get the numbers dialed before I went down. He pointed the taser at Max. Max bared his teeth and looked ready to spring at him like a tiger. I dropped the phone. No way Max would survive a Tasing.

"Good girl," he said and reached for the phone.

Max growled and jumped forward.

"Call the dog off!" he shouted.

"Down Max," I scolded. Max retreated a couple of inches, but continued to growl.

"Arrogant little bastard," he said, kicking at Max.

The phone rang. Charles answered it. "Hello," he said pleasantly. "I'm afraid she is unavailable at the moment. But you can do something for me," he paused and looked out the window. Mark was standing in the street below. "You can stay right where you are and listen if you want to see her again."

Mark stopped in his tracks.

"Good boy. Now tell the old man I want to make a deal, but not here. I'll let him know when. Now listen carefully. Go back inside. Send David out. As soon as he checks in with me, you can have your girlfriend back. If you involve the police, something unfortunate could happen to the girl, and David will go to jail. Do you understand?"

I watched Mark go back inside and David appear a few seconds later. His shirt was torn, and he was limping. He looked towards our building and then turned and headed up the street.

Charles set my phone down and pulled his own from his pocket, dialing. "What the fuck happened to you?" he asked. Then he paused, listening to David's answer on the other end. "A what!" Charles paced around obviously agitated. "You must've got some crazy genes from your mother," he muttered. More pausing. "She said what?" he asked. "All lies. Like usual. Your mother is a liar, kid." He smiled at me.

What a jerk! I mean I know criminals aren't supposed to be nice, but this guy took the cake.

"Just get going," Charles said. "I'll meet you there." He disconnected and looked up at me. "Kids," he said shaking his head.

"You're a jerk," I said.

"I'm going to be a rich jerk, so no one will care."

I turned back towards the window. No sign of anyone.

"Okay," he told me, "this is what's going to happen. You're going to call your boyfriend and tell him you're fine, so he doesn't do anything stupid like call the police. You're going to tell him to stay in the bar until you call him back. And then I'm leaving. Got it?" he asked.

I nodded. Max growled.

Charles handed me my phone. Mark answered on the first ring. "I'm fine," I said. "He wants you to stay inside the bar until he leaves. He said I can call you after he's gone. Is everything okay in there?"

"You wouldn't believe it if I told you," he said. "Are you sure you're okay?"

"Yes, but he has a Taser, and he threatened Max with it."

"Tell Max to rip his balls off if he gets the chance," Mark said grimly.

"Will do," I replied and hung up.

"Thank you for your cooperation," Charles said with an antagonizing smile. "After I leave, count to a hundred slowly. Oh," he said stopping at the door, "and tell big Ed that I'll be in touch real soon and that he'd better bring something a lot bigger than a briefcase to hold my next payment."

Max yipped and growled low in his throat.

"Your dog's got a real attitude problem. If I had more time, I'd teach him a lesson."

I picked Max up and held him against my chest. "Just go!" I shouted as he walked out the door. Max jumped out of my arms and raced for the door. He clawed at it and jumped for the door handle. "Stop it, Max," I said. "Do you want to get killed?" He turned and gave me one of his looks and then ran back over and jumped up on my legs to give me a hug. I waited another minute and then called Mark.

"He's gone, and we're fine," I said walking out the door. "I'm on my way over."

"I'll have a double martini waiting for you," he said.

"I think I'm in love," I said, only half-kidding.

* * *

I left Max in Greene's after promising him extra treats when we got home. He curled up contentedly on an upholstered office chair. Being held hostage was an exhausting affair. McGlynn's was rocking at 10:45 when I walked through the door. Mark rushed forward and wrapped me in his arms. I inhaled eau de Mark and was thankful that the evening had worked out as well as it did.

"Are you okay?" he asked kissing me on the forehead.

"I am now," I said with a sigh. "Where's my drink?"

"At our table. We've got quite a crew," he added as we walked over to two tables that had been put together to accommodate the large group. Carol, Mr. Pyres, and Betty Getty were at one end. Ed and Marcie were at the other.

Ed was consoling Marcie, but stopped long enough to grab my hand and apologize for what happened.

"My poor boy," Marcie wailed. "He's been deceived by that maniac."

I felt her pain. Charles was definitely manipulating David. I relayed what had happened during my temporary hostage crisis.

"See," she said to Ed, "I told you it wasn't his fault."

Well, that's not exactly what I said, but I wasn't looking for a fight. I was looking for a martini. "There was some talk of a martini," I said.

Mark sat a large drink in front of me. "You've earned it," he said. "I've been out of my mind worrying about you with that nut."

I took a drink and said hello to the gang at the other end. It looked like Carol was on drink number two at least. Uh-oh.

"Hello, Mr. Pyres. I'm a little surprised to see you here," I said.

"Why, you told me what a lovely little place this was, so I decided to take Betty here after dinner. And then I saw Ms. Smith and just had to say hello, of course. And then a ruffian at the next table tried to accost the poor woman. I simply had to step in," he said.

"He's my son, not a ruffian," Marcie sobbed at the other end of the table.

"Well, be that as it may, he was not a gentleman," he sniffed.

Marcie said nothing. He had her there.

I checked out Betty Getty. Exactly like her picture. Definitely a librarian.

"Well, I'm so glad you're all right, my dear. We need to be going," The Count said, rising to help Betty up. "I will see you on Monday?"

I nodded.

Betty pulled on her coat. "So nice to meet you, Diana," she said with a shy smile. "Vann told me how you were the one that helped him set up his profile online. You are our Cupid. I never imagined I would meet a man that loved medieval husbandry more than me. He's a gem." She looked at Vann. He beamed.

"One of a kind," I agreed. I took another sip of my drink and shook my head.

Mark leaned over and whispered, "Your vampire kicked David's ass!"

"What? Really?"

Mark nodded barely controlling his laughter. "Apparently David ran him some lip after he stepped in to defend Carol."

Carol raised her glass in acknowledgement and took another gulp. "He spun in a circle and flew through the air and kicked David square in the chest. Sent David into the table behind us like a scene from a bad Western."

"We didn't get in until the fight was over, but David was out like a light," Mark said.

"Some kind of medieval jujitsu, he said. But it looked like vampire moves to me," Carol added and took another drink.

I heard Woody's voice above the den. "I was waiting for you to show up," he yelled and came out from behind the bar. "You and your friends." He shook his head. He seemed a little peeved. "As soon as a crazy guy in a cape starts breakin' bad like Yoda, I should've known he was somehow related to you."

"He's not related to me," I said. "I just work for him. And he was defending Carol."

Woody held up his hand. "I know that's what everybody who saw it said, and that's why I didn't call the police. But come on, Diana. First you're in here with your crazy granddaddy and karaoke Carol over there makin' a scene," Carol didn't even try to defend herself. She just took another gulp of her drink. "Then last night you're in here breakin' up some poor slob's marriage, and now this guy with a cape. What gives?"

"I've had a bad week. That's all," I said glumly.

Everyone nodded their heads. Yep, definitely a bad week. "Need another drink?" he asked, taking pity on me.

"You still want me to play next Friday?" I asked hopefully.

"Sure," he said grabbing my empty glass. "Never a dull moment with you around."

CHAPTER TWENTY-ONE

We spent the next hour waiting to hear from Charles about what his deal for Ed was. I switched to water and persuaded Carol to do like-wise. The consensus was that if there was no word from Charles by noon tomorrow, then Ed would go to the police. Marcie was, of course, opposed to this plan, but Ed was firm for once. There was no other choice. If Charles called, Ed would tell him to name his price to return the data and leave David behind when he left town. Mark had volunteered to take the money and retrieve the data and David. I wasn't happy at all about that.

"This guy is a psychopath," I said again. "He spent ten years in prison. He wouldn't hesitate to kill someone if he had to. It's too dangerous. If you can't call the police, can you hire some professionals?" I asked.

"I'm working on that," Mark said. "My friends overseas recommended some people here, but I'm waiting to hear back." He paused, turning to Carol. "Do you know how they took the data? Emailed it, disc, flash drive?"

Carol nodded. "Flash drive. I saw Charles holding it when he and David were talking."

I felt my stomach do a funny kind of flip. "A sliver flash drive?" I asked.

All eyes turned toward me.

"Yes," Carol responded slowly. "Why?"

"Uh, I *might* have seen that drive," I confessed. I couldn't help the smile that broke out across my face. "And I *might* have already corrupted all of the files on it." For once, my clumsiness pays off!

Mark blinked at me. "You're joking?"

I shook my head, telling him about the drive I'd found in David's office and my little mishap with the software updates. By the time I finished, everyone was wearing grins to match mine. Except Marcie, who just looked like she was going to faint with relief.

"I think that deserves another martini, Queenie Baby," Mark said. Then he leaned in close and whispered in my ear. "You do know how sexy it is that you single handedly saved the day, right?"

I felt shivers run down my spine in a not unpleasant way.

"Diana, I want you to know that you will always have a job with Greene's," Ed broke in, raising his water glass to me.

"So that means you'll be keeping it open?" Carol asked hopefully.

"Well," Ed hedged." I've had my lawyer looking over the lease Marcie signed to David. Quite frankly, it would be a miracle if it held up in court, especially in light of what's been going on there since. Mark's been telling me just what a worthwhile venture the business is after all, but the only problem is that I just don't have the energy anymore to watch over it day to day like it needs. "

"So, you *are* selling?" I asked.

Ed nodded.

I opened my mouth to give him a piece of my mind, but I didn't get the chance.

"I hope," Ed added, with a twinkle in his eye, "to Carol. If she's interested."

Carol looked dumbfounded. Apparently the idea of owning the staffing agency, hadn't occurred to her before. "I'm stunned. I never imagined you'd want me to take over. I don't know what to say."

Ed raised a hand. "Look it's been a long day, and we've still got a mess to untangle here. Take your time and think about. We'll get into the details when things settle down."

Carol nodded. "I really appreciate the offer," she said, still looking a little overwhelmed and unsure.

"Congratulations!" I leaned over at patted her on the back. "This is great."

Ed clapped her on the shoulder. Mark beamed, and I wondered if he'd had something to do with Ed's decision.

Unfortunately, our celebrating was cut short as Ed's phone rang. We all held our breath while he talked. He spoke softly, and I only caught a few words. I heard 'how much' and 'when.' Ed hung up the phone.

"They're on their way to Miami, according to Charles. He wants half a million for the data." He turned to Marcie. "But he has no intention of leaving David behind. He says he needs a partner he can trust, and David fits the bill," Ed said in disgust.

Marcie buried her face in her hands. "I was so afraid of this," she wept.

"Don't worry. I think we can play the fact that they don't know the files are corrupt to our advantage, and get David back." Ed went on to give us the details of the plan, which included Mark heading down to Miami to make the exchange on Monday.

"And why drag me all the way to Miami? Why not do the deal here?" Mark asked ruefully.

"If I had to guess? I think he wants to make sure the data isn't worth more to his original buyer. You need to get down there early tomorrow, before they realize what they have is worthless," Ed said. "We'll keep working on David from our end. Maybe Marcie can get him on the phone again."

Mark and I had no time alone. Mark had to get back to the boat and grab what he could to make a 6:00 a.m. flight out of Reagan National. We scooped up Max and the limo dropped everyone off at their respective places. He left me with a firm kiss on the lips and a promise to call me when he landed in Miami.

I hardly slept that night. I woke to Max sleeping soundly on my chest, and, for once, I didn't make him get down. We had been through a lot yesterday. After a cup of coffee and a long walk with Max, I took a shower and thought about calling Rick. I wanted to hold up my end of the deal. I had promised Mark exclusivity, and I had meant it. I rehearsed what I was going to say over and over and even picked up the phone a couple of times. I chickened out and played my guitar for most of the afternoon. I even lingered over the new song I wrote.

Late in the afternoon, Mark finally called. "I can't get the image of you lying naked on the couch out of my head," he said without preamble.

"So stop trying and get back here so we can pick up where we left off," I replied.

He laughed. "I wish it was that easy." He sighed. "I'm supposed to meet Charles at 9:30 tomorrow morning with the five hundred thousand."

"Where are you meeting?" I asked. The whole thing sounded dangerous.

"At the airport. It seems that Charles hasn't made any friends by trying to up the price on the data. David called Marcie this afternoon, all upset because some thugs were after them. Looks like Charles reneged on his original deal in favor of Ed's half million. Doesn't sound like his first customer is someone you want to cross."

Complete James Bond drama. "This just goes from bad to worse," I said.

"Yeah, but at least I have a shot at getting David to stay. I'm pretty sure Charles is planning on jumping on a plane as soon as I hand him the money. According to Marcie, David is having second thoughts about joining him. I'm hoping to wrap this up tomorrow morning and be on the next plane back."

"I'll be waiting on your couch," I said, adding wickedly, "naked."

We flirted and chatted a few more minutes before hanging up. Now was the time, I told myself, to call Rick. Get it done. Rip the Band-Aid off. I found his number in my phone, but stopped before pushing the button. Why was I hesitant? I was completely falling for Mark. We had a lot in common. He represented the future. Rick was the past. Even the new and improved Rick was still part of the past. I needed to close that door soundly and turn the lock. I eyed my phone. But why did I have this urge to keep the door cracked? Just slightly ajar. In case things didn't work out with Mark? No, if there wasn't a Mark I would still be unsure about Rick. Sure, I would probably be experiencing a lot less sexual frustration right now, but I doubt I would be any more ready to settle down with Rick.

A text saved me from having to make the call. It was from my stepmother's phone, but I doubted it was from her.

Anne: *Send more jerky*

Me: *Is that you Granddaddy?*

Anne: *Yes and send more jerky*

Me: *What are you doing with Anne's phone?*

Anne: *She thinks I'm playing games. But I'm trying to get beer and jerky.*

Me: *I can't help you. Text Dan.*

Anne: *Diana, were you the one that brought him jerky?*

Oops! I didn't respond. Granddaddy was going to have to deal with that one. It was such a beautiful day, that I decided to walk down to one of my favorite little restaurants near the waterfront with outdoor seating. I took my laptop and worked on my website while listening to music. I surfed for some new guitar tabs and checked-in on Facebook. In general I cyber-goofed for a couple of hours, drank iced tea, and ate a salad for dinner. I was just getting ready to shut down my computer when my phone rang.

It was Rick. "Hey, how are you?" I said easily.

"Where are you?" he asked. His voice sounded thick. I heard loud music in the background.

"I'm sitting at a restaurant eating dinner," I said. "How about you?" Again trying to keep it light.

"Alone?" he asked bluntly.

That got my fur up. "Yes, but that's not your concern. You're taking the 'long view,' remember?"

"Yep, that's not workin' for me right now."

"Well, I'm sorry, but it's working just fine for me," I said. His voice sounded really weird. "Are you drunk?" I asked.

"Probably," he said. A boat horn sounded loudly in the distance. I heard the sound a second later through the phone.

Oh, no. "Are you in Annapolis?" I asked.

Hesitation on the other end. "Yep."

"Where?" I asked with dread.

"Sitting on your front porch waiting for you."

"You drove drunk over here from Dover?" I asked incredulously.

"No, I brought you a bottle of Jack and an Alicia Keys CD. When you weren't here, I waited awhile and then started imagining all sorts of things. I took a few sips of Jack and put in the CD. Now the bottle's empty, and I'm sittin' on your front step and that fuckin' CD is stuck!" he screamed at the top of his lungs, presumably in the direction of his truck. I could hear Alicia Keys blaring in the background.

"Go turn the CD off and find someplace to throw the bottle away. My neighbor's going to call the police on you," I said waving my hand to the waitress to get the check.

"Nope. She said she wasn't callin' the police because they'd put her back in the funny farm. She's going to shoot me instead as soon as she can get her gun loaded," he said with a drunken laugh.

"What!" I shrieked. Holy moly! Mrs. Kester was definitely off her rocker. I was running back up the street trying to keep the phone to my ear and hold onto my laptop. "Turn the music off at least," I shouted into the phone.

"Can't—I told you," he slurred, "It's stuck, and it's full blast. It just keeps playing that fuckin' song over and over again. I rolled up the windows, but I can still hear it. It's like I'm dead, and this is Hell," he fumed.

I stuffed the phone back in my purse and picked up the pace. One block over I could clearly hear Alicia Keys singing "Fallin'." The thumping through the closed windows of the truck was impressive. I rounded the corner and saw Rick sprawled out on my front porch holding his hands to his ears.

"It's not loud enough that you have to hold your ears," I said giving him a kick.

He sat up and gave me a drunken smile. "It is when you've heard it thirty times. You just get prettier every time I see you, you know that?" he said like a little boy.

Rick was a charming drunk. I remembered that from the few times it had happened in high school. He also got real friendly.

"Come here and give me some sugar," he said doing a fair imitation of Granddaddy trying to make time with the nurses at the hospital.

He made a grab for me and caught me around the knees. I fell forward, managing to drop my laptop into the bushes instead of the concrete. "Let me go, Rick," I said. Alicia Keys blared in the background.

"I keep on fallin' in and outta love with you, Diana," he said softly.

This might have been romantic if he hadn't been drunk and we weren't sprawled out on the front steps in broad daylight.

"Let's go up to my condo," I said still trying to wiggle out of his grasp.

"Now you're talking," he murmured against my lips. The song started again.

Mrs. Kester's front window suddenly swung open. Jesus, I had forgotten about the gun. She leaned out the window and screamed, "Couldn't get my gun loaded, but this should cool you two alley cats off!"

A blast of spray from a garden hose hit me square in the face. I held up my hands and tried to turn away. She leaned out the window and started in on Rick. He howled with laughter. She kept screaming, "This will cool you off, you nasty drunk!"

We were both drenched when Mrs. Kester finally turned off the hose and slammed her window shut. The song continued to play. I think Rick was right. I must have died, and I was doing time in Hell.

He looked up at me and said, "I can see your nipples through your shirt."

"Thanks for noticing," I said and dug for my keys. Step one, get the drunk off the porch. Step two, get changed. Step three, blow up the truck to stop the music.

It was almost dark by the time I got through all the steps. Instead of blowing up the truck I unhooked the battery. I figured if the song kept going after that, then we really were in Hell. Rick was shirtless and sprawled out asleep on my bed. It had taken quite an effort to get him up the stairs and reasonably dry before dumping him there. It also took quite a bit of effort to keep from being dragged into the bed, even in his current inebriated state. I had changed into a comfy sweat suit and confirmed that my laptop was still functioning. After checking my phone, I found I had missed a call from Mark.

"Hey, I miss you," he said in a tone that made me smile.

"Me too," I replied.

"I have a meeting scheduled tonight with some private security people my friends overseas recommended. Hopefully they can give me some backup when I meet Charles tomorrow morning." I could hear the tiredness in his voice. "I'll call you after and let you know how it went. Can't wait to see you again. Naked or otherwise," he added before hanging up.

I smiled at the phone for a few seconds like a school girl getting her first call from a boy, and then I breathed a sigh of relief. No need to complicate things any more than they already were.

Max was curled up in his doggy bed, oblivious to my dilemma.

I made myself a snack and stared mindlessly at the TV for an hour. I heard Rick get up, go to the bathroom and then fall back into my bed. Apparently, I would be sleeping on the couch tonight. Tomorrow morning my plan was to get Rick up and out the door first thing while working in a speech about how I didn't see a future for us. It was all in the past as far as I was concerned.

A lot to do for a Monday morning.

CHAPTER TWENTY-TWO

———

I jolted awake. My mind was fuzzy from staying up too late watching TV and listening to Rick snore in the other room. It was after 9:00. I had to get to work. And get Rick out of here. And break up with him. And pray that nothing bad happened to Mark during the exchange. And also make sure Mark didn't call in the middle of it all. I hate Mondays!

Rick was up and in the shower when I ran into the bedroom and started digging through my closet. I heard the water turn off just as I was pulling on fresh underwear. It wouldn't set the right breaking-things-off-with-you tone if he came in, and I was bottomless. I was just buttoning my shirt when he emerged from the bathroom. He looked fresh and rested with a towel wrapped loosely around his hips. Water drops still clung to his chest. I had to shake myself not to stare. This was too much temptation.

"Darn!" he said. "If I'd have just been a few seconds earlier." He started moving towards me.

I held up my hand to ward him off. "Not so fast," I said firmly. "I have to be at work at 10:00, and you need to go. Last night was not pretty. Jesus, Rick, my neighbor threatened to shoot you."

Rick hung his head. "So all that actually happened, huh?" he asked, sitting down on my bed. "I was hoping it was just a bad dream that ended with us in this bed together." He looked up hopefully.

"Not a chance," I said.

"I'm sorry, Diana," Rick said letting out a deep breath. "I got some news yesterday, and even though I was expecting it, I still got blindsided. I came here thinking that if I could see you and touch you it would make everything all right." He shook his head. "Then you weren't here when I got here, and my mind went wild with all kinds of scenarios. It was an unfortunate time to find myself alone with time on my hands and a bottle of Jack."

"Yeah, the Jack you were planning to use on me," I said, but with less heat.

He smiled. "Well, the Jack and the CD kind of backfired on me. So I guess I got what was coming to me for ditching my 'take the long view' plan. Did that song really play over and over again? Or did I dream it?"

I nodded. "It played until I disconnected your battery. And you'd be sitting in jail right now if Mrs. Kester hadn't been afraid of calling the police again."

"She's a mean one. Can't believe she turned the hose on us," he said in amusement.

"Well, it's not funny to me. I have to live here, remember?" I said putting my hands on my hips.

"I love it when you get fired up," he said and tried to pull me between his knees.

I jumped back. "No! That's not happening. And there's no point in having a 'long view.' We aren't meant to be together, Rick. I'm seeing Mark exclusively, and I don't want you thinking of me like this anymore." There, it was out. I thought I would feel instant relief, but I only felt sad as Rick lowered his head to his hands. As I reached the door, I turned and asked, "What was your news, Rick? What made you come all the way over here to see me?"

He lifted his head up and held my eye. "My divorce is final. Found the papers in the mailbox," he said softly.

"I'm sorry," I said ineffectually. "I'm sorry about all of this."

I left the room, so he could get dressed. I went into the kitchen and made coffee. Max looked at his empty bowl and at the door. I could almost hear his snooty dog voice saying, "Late again, you slacker."

Rick came out and grabbed his keys and wallet off the table.

"Do you want some coffee?" I asked. "It'll be ready in a couple of minutes."

He looked at me and smiled. "I'm not sure my stomach can handle your witch's brew."

"Hey," I said indignantly, "my coffee is good."

"Didn't used to be," he said with a grimace.

"I was a teenager, and that was twelve years ago, Rick. I can make a decent cup of coffee now."

"I'll try your coffee," he said. "I like to think people can change."

I saw where he was going with this but didn't say anything. "Want me to take your dog out for you?" he asked.

Max looked from him to me.

"Sure," I said.

I scooped up my purse and grabbed my phone off the charger. Uh-oh. I had missed two texts last night.

Mark: *Just found out they left town. Going to Puerto Rico. Getting on a flight at midnight. Call you in the morning.*

Mark: *I miss you.*

Before I could process anything, my phone rang. Not Mark, was my first thought. I didn't recognize the number, but I decided to answer it.

"Diana? It's Mark," he said, sounding happy to talk to me.

Oh, no! Maybe if I just hung up. "Hi, Mark," I replied like an idiot. "Where are you calling from?"

"A phone in the lobby of the hotel I'm staying at. My phone is dead, and I forgot my charger. I'm on my way to get one now, but I had to call you," he said with excitement.

"Oh, that's so sweet," I said trying to hurry him off the phone, "but I really need to get to work. Can I call you back at 1:00?" I heard footsteps on the stairs.

"No," he said with a laugh, "I'm not calling to be sweet. I'm calling because something bizarre just happened."

The door was opening. Max bounded into the kitchen looking for his food. I heard Rick say something about 'finally getting that damned CD out'.

"What about Charles and David?" I asked to cover the noise.

"No word. Nothing. All I know is they must have changed their mind about dealing with Ed, as they left Miami last night. They arrived here in Puerto Rico about nine hours ahead of me. But what I called to tell you was that I just heard your song."

Rick walked in and hung up Max's leash. I held up my hand.

"What did you say?" I asked.

"I said I heard your song. Here—in Puerto Rico on a radio station," he said.

"You heard my song? On the radio?" I said loudly, causing Rick to look up.

"Yes," he said, "'The Rum Song.' A man was singing it, but I recognized it as soon as I heard it. Any idea what's going on?"

"They stole my song!" I shrieked. "Those bastards stole my song."

Rick came up behind me. "What's wrong?" he asked.

There was a pause at the other end. "Is that Rick?" Mark asked incredulously.

I thought about making buzzing noises to fake static, but I guess I waited too long, because Mark said, "Don't act like you can't hear me, and don't hang up on me either," he barked. "What the hell, Diana? What about the whole 'exclusivity' thing? Did you just throw that out the window?"

"Nothing happened. Rick was on my doorstep when I came back from dinner. He just got his divorce papers, and he was looking for a shoulder to cry on. That was it," I said quickly. I motioned to Rick to come over. He had a big smile on his face. I covered the phone. "Don't you do this!" I whispered furiously at him. "You tell the truth!"

"That doesn't explain what he's still doing at your place," Mark said between clenched teeth. "I can't take this right now, Diana. I'm chasing a nut around who may or may not have hired thugs hunting for him. I don't speak Spanish, and these people drive like New York cab drivers. How much more can I take?" I was pretty sure his eyes were bulging out of their sockets on the other end of the phone.

"He was drunk when I got here. I slept on the couch, and this morning I told him that you and I are exclusive," I waved to Rick encouragingly, "Tell him Rick."

He stared at me a second and then shook his head like he couldn't believe he was doing this. "She's all yours, man," he said loudly. "Treat her good."

"Great," Mark said sarcastically, "the guy you spent the night with—for the second time this week, I might add—says you're all mine. I have warm fuzzies."

"Mark," I said trying again, "I am sorry. I know this looks bad."

Rick motioned for me to hand him the phone. I made a face. He waved again. I shook my head in defeat and handed him the phone.

"Mark. Just listen, man," Rick said calmly. "I know you're hot under the collar about being thousands of miles away while your sexy, new girlfriend is having sleepovers with her old boyfriend."

"Not helping!" I growled.

"Anyway," Rick continued, "this is simple. The question is this: do you really think if I just spent last night in bed with Diana, who happens to be the one true love of my life, that I would be having this conversation? I'm a tolerant man, but that ain't going to happen."

I motioned for the phone back. Rick waved me away. "Why? Because I'm not the same guy I used to be, and I want her to know that," Rick said and then paused listening to Mark. "Well, you got me on that one," Rick said with a laugh. He handed me back the phone. "Smart guy," he said. "Said, 'yeah, and you're earning brownie points for when I fuck this up.'"

"There are no brownie points!" I said and grabbed the phone back. "I'm sorry about all this, Mark. It has all been a fantastic comedy of errors."

"I'm pretty sure most of your life is a 'fantastic comedy of errors,'" he said wryly. "But if it hadn't been for all the craziness, we would've never met. So I guess I just have to get used to it. Rick seems like a good guy. Too bad he's trying to steal you away from me. I think we could have been friends otherwise. Maybe I should fix him up with my sister."

"So…" I prodded. "Are we okay?"

"I think we could be more than okay," he said.

"Yeah? How?" I asked watching Rick pour himself a cup of coffee.

"Grab your bikini and get on a plane. We'll chase bad guys, figure out who stole your song, and get naked. But definitely not in that order," he said like the pied piper luring me away.

A million 'I can'ts' filled my head. Max. Work. Gigs. "Okay," I said suddenly. "I'll go."

Rick rolled his eyes and took a swig of coffee. I said goodbye to Mark and promised to call at lunch when I had a chance to work out the details.

Rick watched me closely as I flitted around the room getting ready to leave for work. "Puerto Rico, huh?" he asked shaking his head. "That guy *so* owes me."

"Thank you so much," I said earnestly. "And about what you said to Mark. You're right you're not the guy you used to be."

"But still not the right guy for you," he said with a sigh.

I looked up at him sadly and shook my head no.

He took another sip of coffee and grimaced. "Some things don't change. Your coffee still sucks."

Okay so maybe my coffee did still suck. But I felt like I had changed in the last week. I'd saved Green's staffing from disaster, held my own in a hostage situation, and even managed to find love for a vampire. Not to mention my own new love to explore. An old love resolved. A trip to Puerto Rico on the horizon. Life was looking up.

"Hey," Rick yelled, banging angrily on my window. "What's that crazy old lady rubbing all over my truck!"

I glanced out the window. Yuck. "Did Max poop when you took him out?" I asked.

"Yeah, so?" he answered banging on the window again. Mrs. Kester turned around and gave him the finger.

"You didn't use a baggy, did you?" I asked. Rick cursed.

Maybe I needed a real estate agent, too.

ABOUT THE AUTHOR

Christina Burke wrote her first novel more than twenty years ago. Life and career took over until she found her way back to fiction writing through the unlikely avenue of metastatic breast cancer. Among other business and education credentials, she holds a Doctorate in Business Administration. Christina, her husband, Jim, and their two children live in Dover, Delaware with the family sidekick, Max the Wonder Dog.

To learn more about Christina, visit her online at
www.caburke.com

Enjoyed this book? Check out these other fun and fabulous reads available in print now from Gemma Halliday Publishing:

www.GemmaHalliday.com/Halliday_Publishing

Made in the USA
Lexington, KY
27 May 2015